Killer's Law

SELECTED FICTION WORKS BY
L. RON HUBBARD

FANTASY
The Case of the Friendly Corpse

Death's Deputy

Fear

The Ghoul

The Indigestible Triton

Slaves of Sleep & The Masters of Sleep

Typewriter in the Sky

The Ultimate Adventure

SCIENCE FICTION
Battlefield Earth

The Conquest of Space

The End Is Not Yet

Final Blackout

The Kilkenny Cats

The Kingslayer

The Mission Earth Dekalogy*

Ole Doc Methuselah

To the Stars

ADVENTURE
The Hell Job series

WESTERN
Buckskin Brigades

Empty Saddles

Guns of Mark Jardine

Hot Lead Payoff

A full list of L. Ron Hubbard's
novellas and short stories is provided at the back.

*Dekalogy—a group of ten volumes

L. RON HUBBARD

Killer's Law

GALAXY PRESS

Published by
Galaxy Press, LLC
7051 Hollywood Boulevard, Suite 200
Hollywood, CA 90028

Printed in the United States of America.

ISBN-10   1-59212-287-6
ISBN-13   978-1-59212-287-5

Library of Congress Control Number: 2007928124

Contents

Stories from Pulp Fiction's Golden Age

A ND it *was* a golden age.
The 1930s and 1940s were a vibrant, seminal time for a gigantic audience of eager readers, probably the largest per capita audience of readers in American history. The magazine racks were chock-full of publications with ragged trims, garish cover art, cheap brown pulp paper, low cover prices—and the most excitement you could hold in your hands.

"Pulp" magazines, named for their rough-cut, pulpwood paper, were a vehicle for more amazing tales than Scheherazade could have told in a million and one nights. Set apart from higher-class "slick" magazines, printed on fancy glossy paper with quality artwork and superior production values, the pulps were for the "rest of us," adventure story after adventure story for people who liked to *read*. Pulp fiction authors were no-holds-barred entertainers—real storytellers. They were more interested in a thrilling plot twist, a horrific villain or a white-knuckle adventure than they were in lavish prose or convoluted metaphors.

The sheer volume of tales released during this wondrous golden age remains unmatched in any other period of literary history—hundreds of thousands of published stories in over nine hundred different magazines. Some titles lasted only an issue or two; many magazines succumbed to paper shortages during World War II, while others endured for decades yet. Pulp fiction remains as a treasure trove of stories you can read, stories you can love, stories you can remember. The stories were driven by plot and character, with grand heroes, terrible villains, beautiful damsels (often in distress), diabolical plots, amazing places, breathless romances. The readers wanted to be taken beyond the mundane, to live adventures far removed from their ordinary lives—and the pulps rarely failed to deliver.

In that regard, pulp fiction stands in the tradition of all memorable literature. For as history has shown, good stories are much more than fancy prose. William Shakespeare, Charles Dickens, Jules Verne, Alexandre Dumas—many of the greatest literary figures wrote their fiction for the readers, not simply literary colleagues and academic admirers. And writers for pulp magazines were no exception. These publications reached an audience that dwarfed the circulations of today's short story magazines. Issues of the pulps were scooped up and read by over thirty million avid readers each month.

Because pulp fiction writers were often paid no more than a cent a word, they had to become prolific or starve. They also had to write aggressively. As Richard Kyle, publisher and editor of *Argosy,* the first and most long-lived of the pulps, so pointedly explained: "The pulp magazine writers, the best of them, worked for markets that did not write for critics or attempt to satisfy timid advertisers. Not having to answer to anyone other than their readers, they wrote about human beings on the edges of the unknown, in those new lands the future would explore. They wrote for what we would become, not for what we had already been."

Some of the more lasting names that graced the pulps include H. P. Lovecraft, Edgar Rice Burroughs, Robert E. Howard, Max Brand, Louis L'Amour, Elmore Leonard, Dashiell Hammett, Raymond Chandler, Erle Stanley Gardner, John D. MacDonald, Ray Bradbury, Isaac Asimov, Robert Heinlein—and, of course, L. Ron Hubbard.

In a word, he was among the most prolific and popular writers of the era. He was also the most enduring—hence this series—and certainly among the most legendary. It all began only months after he first tried his hand at fiction, with L. Ron Hubbard tales appearing in *Thrilling Adventures, Argosy, Five-Novels Monthly, Detective Fiction Weekly, Top-Notch, Texas Ranger, War Birds, Western Stories,* even *Romantic Range.* He could write on any subject, in any genre, from jungle explorers to deep-sea divers, from G-men and gangsters, cowboys and flying aces to mountain climbers, hard-boiled detectives and spies. But he really began to shine when he turned his talent to science fiction and fantasy of which he authored nearly fifty novels or novelettes to forever change the shape of those genres.

Following in the tradition of such famed authors as Herman Melville, Mark Twain, Jack London and Ernest Hemingway, Ron Hubbard actually lived adventures that his own characters would have admired—as an ethnologist among primitive tribes, as prospector and engineer in hostile climes, as a captain of vessels on four oceans. He even wrote a series of articles for *Argosy*, called "Hell Job," in which he lived and told of the most dangerous professions a man could put his hand to.

Finally, and just for good measure, he was also an accomplished photographer, artist, filmmaker, musician and educator. But he was first and foremost a *writer*, and that's the L. Ron Hubbard we come to know through the pages of this volume.

This library of Stories from the Golden Age presents the best of L. Ron Hubbard's fiction from the heyday of storytelling, the Golden Age of the pulp magazines. In these eighty volumes, readers are treated to a full banquet of 153 stories, a kaleidoscope of tales representing every imaginable genre: science fiction, fantasy, western, mystery, thriller, horror, even romance—action of all kinds and in all places.

Because the pulps themselves were printed on such inexpensive paper with high acid content, issues were not meant to endure. As the years go by, the original issues of every pulp from *Argosy* through *Zeppelin Stories* continue crumbling into brittle, brown dust. This library preserves the L. Ron Hubbard tales from that era, presented with a distinctive look that brings back the nostalgic flavor of those times.

L. Ron Hubbard's Stories from the Golden Age has something for every taste, every reader. These tales will return you to a time when fiction was good clean entertainment and the most fun a kid could have on a rainy afternoon or the best thing an adult could enjoy after a long day at work.

Pick up a volume, and remember what reading is supposed to be all about. Remember curling up with a *great story.*

—Kevin J. Anderson

KEVIN J. ANDERSON *is the author of more than ninety critically acclaimed works of speculative fiction, including The Saga of Seven Suns, the continuation of the Dune Chronicles with Brian Herbert, and his* New York Times *bestselling novelization of L. Ron Hubbard's* Ai! Pedrito!

Killer's Law

Killer's Law

WHEN Kyle stepped off the Capitol Limited and into the confused fury of Washington, a headline caught his glance:

SENATOR MORRAN BEGINS
COPPER QUIZ

A few hours from now, his own name would be blazing there, black as the ink in which it would be printed. Kyle knew nothing of prophecy; his interest was in getting through this stampede of people and completing his mission. Already he was creating a mild sensation. Palo Alto hat, silver thong, scarlet kerchief, high-heeled boots and his six feet three of gawky, bony height commanded attention.

He stood for a moment in the crowded, clanging dusk, looking toward the lighted dome of the Capitol, trying without much success to savor the scene and feel patriotic. A redcap, eyeing his huge bag now that Kyle had dragged it all the way through the station from the train, swooped down with confidence born of the stranger's obvious confusion. The action met abruptly explosive resistance.

Kyle said, "Hands off."

The redcap retained his hold as a legal right to a tip. Kyle gave the handle a twist which sent him reeling. A few people paused to watch.

A cop said, "What's the matter here? Keep moving, you."

Kyle said testily, "Move along, hell. I'm Sheriff Kyle of Deadeye, Nevada, and I got an appointment to meet Senator Morran—"

"Yeah?" the cop said.

"Could I be of assistance?" said a smooth-faced gentleman. "Your name, I think, is Kyle. Senator Morran sent me down to meet you." He laughed good-naturedly and nodded to the cop. "That's all right, Officer."

The cop was satisfied. The redcap departed without tip.

"My name is Johnson, Sheriff," the smooth-faced man said. "John Johnson. Just call me Johnny." He laughed. "And now we'll see about getting you to the senator."

"Hold it," Kyle said. "How do I know who you are?" He had to bend over to look at Johnson. He did so and said, "Why don't you just run along and tell the senator I'll be with him soon. I'm taking a cab."

"Well—" Johnson turned toward a waiting limousine and Kyle's glance collided with the chauffeur's. He moved away while Johnson still hesitated, and hailed a cab.

"Soreham Hotel," he told the driver.

The Soreham Hotel was lighted in every window, its walks aglitter with dinner gowns, its lobby thick with political cigar smoke and the aura of martinis. Kyle asked the desk clerk for the senator's room number and a house phone.

The phone didn't answer. He went up.

Senator Morran's room was 310. Its door, open to darkness,

surprised Kyle. The faint hall light reached poorly into the room, but showed a dark, irregular streak, running jaggedly along the floor.

Kyle was in the act of stepping backward when the room exploded into Roman candle brilliance. The pain came fractionally later, just as the lights careened out again. His last conscious impression was of himself, trying to push the floor away with his hands.

They shook him into light and sound and cuffed him into attention, and though it took seven of them, they held him in the chair.

The room was a flood of sound, a maelstrom of confusion. Reporters were surging against a police cordon at the door. Politicians, bloodhounding newsprint, were issuing statements. Flashbulbs were bursting. And the center of attention, Kyle noted, as he had always been in life, was the senator.

The silver mane which had thrilled women voters for two decades was in noble repose, except at the ends where it was darkly matted. The strength, the nobility of pose were gone, and the hands, which in their youth had bulldogged many a steer and later had been lifted in appeal to many a constituent, were motionless, expressionless—their mute story told by a heavy candlestick lying beside them.

In the upper abdomen a knife hilt was visible.

Kyle's feelings shut out the sounds about him. He had known Senator Morran well. The old man, as much as anything, had won him his job. He had always regarded Morran as a staunch, friendly and fearless warrior for the things he himself believed in. He had come too far to be welcomed by this, and suddenly Kyle felt alone and sick.

He realized the desk clerk was pointing him out and a flashbulb battered at him. Somebody asked, "Why did you kill him, mister?" and he awoke to the fact that this question had been thudding into him for five full minutes. The realization choked him.

"His knife, all right," somebody said. "See? Matches the empty sheath. Five-inch blade. Five-inch hole. Fits."

"Why did you kill Senator Morran?"

"Damn you," Kyle said. "Get the hell away from me. I didn't kill him!"

"Why did you kill Senator Morran?"

He tried to get up but they thrust him roughly back. "Here. Here, look in my pockets. He wired—"

"We looked." They waited then.

Kyle said, "I'm Sheriff Kyle from Deadeye. He wired me, had me bring him some documents. I brought my bag straight to—" He stopped, stared around the room. "Where's my bag?" he howled at them.

It took three of them to get him back into the chair. "We'll find the bag," said the detective. "First we want to know why you killed Senator Morran."

Rage was beginning to rise in him, but he held it in check. He sat still until they stopped asking him. He watched a reporter, hat uptilted, cigarette dangling, who had an illusion about solving murders himself, get told off.

"Get out of here, Mike!" snarled a detective.

"So you got a monopoly on questions, Haggerty," said the

reporter, and wandered over and stared down at the corpse. He was making sympathetic noises with his tongue when the late senator's secretary arrived.

Mike said, "Hey, Cronin! If you're through playing with this stiff, cover it up. Can't you see we got ladies present?"

Somebody draped a sheet over the senator, leaving one matted lock of gray hair, one gray hand showing.

"What was the senator doing today to cause all this, miss?" Mike asked.

The woman moaned something and Kyle stared at her. He knew most of the senator's employees in a vague way, for they had accompanied him West from time to time. But he did not know this girl.

"Just his regular work," she sobbed.

"How about the copper investigation?" said Mike. "I understand he was starting on that tomorrow?"

"Yes—but he had nothing on anyone really."

"I heard," said Mike, "that he sent West for some records."

"Who—oh, I don't think so."

"This puncher here claims he was bringing records East to the senator. What do you know?"

"Oh, no. I don't think so. I never saw this man before in my life. But—someone threatened Senator Morran yesterday."

Mike said, "How did he do this?"

"By telephone. He said he was going to 'get' the senator. I heard the whole conversation on my own phone."

Mike grinned. "There you are, Haggerty. Open and shut. Threat, murder. Let the sheriff speak, so she can identify the voice. What's your name, miss?"

"Annie Molyneaux."

"You live at—"

"The Jacob Arms Apartments."

Mike grinned, closed his notebook and went outside to telephone.

Haggerty unlocked Kyle from the chair and, with three brawny flatfeet, took him through the crowd and down to the waiting wagon. Kyle went meekly enough until he caught sight of Jules Harmon.

Kyle had met the copper king on several occasions. The man had come to Nevada during the late boom, had bought out smaller operators, had exploited supposedly worked-out mines and had gained himself vast riches and power.

"Mr. Harmon," he said.

Harmon looked away.

They had Kyle on the steps of the Black Maria, when it happened. A small round object fell at his feet. There was a dull explosion. From the pavement long smoky fingers burst and leaped. They coiled and rose and spread and Kyle reacted to the released pressure on him to whirl free and strike with pent-up ferocity.

He sprang ahead through the yellow mist, blind but determined. He crashed into a wall, rebounded, detoured, plunged on. The slope was descending and he let it guide him. Light was pale stuff through his suffering gaze. There were shouts behind him and these too he used for a guide. At any instant he expected bullets to thud into him and when he collided with a bush and fell, he thought for an instant a slug had done it. He rolled and found himself clear of the gas.

His eyes tearing, he came to his knees. The hotel was a hundred yards up the slope from him. Bedlam was bursting from the place. Kyle looked down. He did not know Washington well enough to understand that he was gazing at Rock Creek Park, hundreds of acres of wild land in a deep and craggy ravine, but he did comprehend that here was sanctuary he could find his way in.

On hands and knees he scrambled down into the dark abyss, expertly using cover, traveling soundlessly as a fox. He paused once to listen and examine the gun he'd managed to wrest from one of the cops. There was shouting somewhere, at different places where they sought to form a cordon.

Kyle hugged earth and went deeper into the wilderness.

He had carefully cached his hat and boots in a tree, forty dollars' worth of Stetson, well out of sight. He had found a drunk, sleeping it off in a car, and had borrowed a black overcoat, shoes and hat. He had made his way up a steep bank and into the backyard of a house far from the Soreham. He had left a hundred cops floundering through darkness and ruining shrubbery. And at 2:15 AM he was knocking on the door of apartment 21, Jacob Arms.

Annie Molyneaux was up. Gowned in something dark and lacy, she answered the door, then tried to slam it.

Kyle forced his way in. After a look at his face she thought better of screaming.

"What . . . what do you want?"

"As much as you can tell me," Kyle said. "To start with—where can I find a man who calls himself Johnny Johnson?"

Her gaze was blank.

"An oily man, so high. He knew I was coming. The senator wouldn't have told him. Did you?"

She wasn't blank now. She was caught. Kyle put aside his gallantry, and from a recess in his clothing the police hadn't had time to examine, he produced a knife. Back home he'd always carried a hideaway for emergencies.

She squirmed and when she looked at him again the knife blade was in front of her.

"Where can I find him?"

She stared at the knife, hypnotized.

"Johansen. Martin Johansen," she said.

"What's his address?"

"I . . . I won't . . ."

He saw her telephone number book and scooped it up. Johansen was listed as 3028 P Street, NW.

He did not want to tie her, but he had to, using an extension cord and a towel for a gag. She was docile enough. Evidently she had not expected to be allowed to live.

Cautiously Kyle slid out into the hall, found it deserted and closed her door. The operator at the switchboard was still asleep—it was not until he had gained the street that he met danger. A roadster had just pulled up to the curb and a white sign on the windshield said: PRESS.

*Kyle put aside his gallantry, and from a recess in his
clothing the police hadn't had time to examine,
he produced a knife.*

Kyle could have ducked into the entrance and taken his chances. He did not. The street was otherwise uninhabited and he needed transportation. When Mike Strible started to get out, a glittering knife drove him back.

"Be quiet and do as you are told," Kyle said. "Get under that wheel."

Recognition chilled the reporter. He slid back under the wheel and Kyle gave him Martin Johansen's address.

"Okay," Mike said.

Kyle asked after a while, "Put my name in the papers, didn't you? What did you say?"

Mike said, "What it was my job to say. That's all I was doing."

"Well, do some more of it. Stay with me and you'll have the rest of your story."

"I can't be forced—"

"No?" Kyle asked, and Mike glanced obliquely at the knife and drove.

At 3028 P Street, NW, a woman blinked at them through a slit-opened door and gave them an argument. A second-floor window jumped open.

The man who had called himself Johnny Johnson, and who was Martin Johansen, thrust a head and nightgowned shoulders out over the street.

"Who's down there?"

"You answer," hissed Kyle.

Mike gave his name. "A tip you'll want to buy, Martin," he said.

"I'll be down," said Johansen.

12

In a couple of minutes he came down, shrugging into a topcoat. He paid no attention to the woman and came out into the street.

The first intimation he had that all was not well was a knife blade digging at his back.

"Get in the car," Kyle told him.

Johansen, shaking now, got in. He recognized Kyle suddenly and swore.

Kyle said, "Take us to two-twenty Rondel Road, Chevy Chase, Mike."

Jules Harmon came awake with a start. His sleep had been restless and it took him a moment to realize that a sound somewhere in the vast dimensions of his home had roused him.

For reasons of his own he was alone tonight—even the servants were away. On such occasions he generally kept a gun in his bedroom, against possible intruders. He armed himself now and went downstairs.

There was a creak on the porch, a soft slither as the knob of the front door turned. Harmon quietly swept back a curtain to admit moonlight and then cloaked himself in a drape. He waited.

Several minutes passed. There was no further sound from the porch or the door. Evidently the intruder had yielded to the lock. Harmon cursed the accident that tonight, of all nights, he did not care to call the police.

The quiet became oppressive. Harmon had never realized how isolated this house was. He could not even hear the sparse traffic of Wisconsin Avenue. It surprised him that his hand was trembling. Moonlight had never looked this chilly and white to him.

There was a creak upstairs. Harmon began to sweat. Somehow the fellow had gained entrance in the rear of the house. Harmon came out of concealment and, accidentally, knocked over a floor lamp.

The noise magnified itself as it tumbled through the dark house. Harmon fumbled behind him for the main light switch, found and held it. When the intruder came down he would flick the switch and shoot.

There were footfalls in the hall, a threatening whisper and then a board at the top of the landing creaked. Harmon's fingers tightened on the wall switch.

His attention was momentarily distracted by a thin wail on Wisconsin Avenue. A police car en route somewhere. He began to sweat a little. Shooting the intruder would mean that he would have to call the police—but maybe by then it would be all right.

He steadied his gun hand, raised the weapon. He drowned the room with light and fired in nearly the same instant. He turned off the lights and the blaze of them still danced in the darkness about him.

There was a soft slithering sound, a moan rose as the echoes of the shots died away. Harmon's brain resolved the image on the landing into two figures. The slithering persisted and then something crashed into a chair in the living room. Harmon grinned with satisfaction.

He changed his position to the other side of the switch, now protected by the chair. But there was no answering shot.

The screaming siren grew louder and louder, cutting into Harmon's tension. He realized with a start that the car was coming here, that even now it was drawing up in front of the house and screaming to a stop.

A soft footfall seemed to come from the stairs. Harmon knew now he must end this instantly. He plunged on the lights, rapidly swung his gun in search of his target.

A mighty arm seized him from behind, wound tensely about his throat, twisting his spinal column into a shaft of crimson agony. He fired wildly as a reflex.

When he sought to lift his gun, a glittering knife edge slashed his wrist and the .38 clattered to the hardwood floor.

Shoulders were crashing into the main door and Kyle thought fast. By the moonlight he could see the dining room beyond an alcove. Dragging Harmon with him, he backed away from the fury which assaulted the door and took position in the darkness. He kicked chairs out of his way and heaved up one end of the dining table to use as a barricade.

The hinges and lock gave way simultaneously and light, anger and guns avalanched into the living room.

Haggerty found the light switch and all motion ceased under the glare. Johansen was lying in the remains of a smashed chair, spattered with blood, twitching.

With a glance around, Haggerty stepped toward the dying man.

"All right, Haggerty—far enough." Kyle crouched behind his bastion, showing nothing more than his right eye and a gun.

A soft footfall seemed to come from the stairs. Harmon knew now he must end this instantly. He plunged on the lights, rapidly swung his gun in search of his target.

They froze. Two of the police were accommodating enough to drop their guns, unasked, upon the floor. Haggerty began to turn a light violet.

"Keep away from that door," Kyle said. "I got a friend here you'll be very interested in shortly."

He thrust the lower half of Harmon into view by exerting a little expert pressure on his spinal column.

"Harmon here shot the gent you see in there. That's Harmon's gun and the bullets ought to match. Most likely he had a license to carry it."

"He ain't dead?" growled Haggerty.

"No," Kyle said. "He'll save me breath. Harmon was about to be exposed by Senator Morran for war profits, and he hired that gent Johansen to kill him. Johansen found out about my bringing Morran's records from Annie Molyneaux—you'll find her tied up in her own apartment and plenty ready to confess, I think. And you'll find my bag upstairs, with the records."

Haggerty was uncertain. But Kyle's position carried persuasion.

He asked, "Who tossed that gas bomb that let you get away?"

"My guess would be Harmon. He knew I'd look him up. Maybe he thought he could buy or scare me off. He knew you couldn't hold me long on murder. Or maybe he hoped you'd shoot me dead."

"This Johansen—wait a minute." Haggerty leaned over the dying man. "Listen, you. Did you kill Morran? You're dying, see? Don't you want to get it off your conscience? Did you kill Morran?"

Kyle could see the concentration it cost the murderer to answer. He did not even hear the formed yes but he saw the weak nod. Froth and blood bubbled through Johansen's mouth. The effort finished him.

Kyle let go of Harmon. It was a mistake. Haggerty was not yet ready to take him over, and Harmon took advantage of a moment's hesitation on the part of the police.

He dived backwards through the door into the kitchen and was gone. Kyle started in pursuit, but realized his own position. He was not yet in the clear. He swung around, transferring his gun back to the right hand. "Stay where you are. He won't get far. What I want to know is, am I held or not?"

"Well—" said Haggerty, "as a material witness—"

"Mike," Kyle called.

The reporter showed in the doorway.

Kyle said, "You've got the story I promised you. You'll give me full credit, huh?"

"Sure," Mike grinned.

Haggerty squirmed.

A commotion sounded on the front steps. A cop who had been left to guard outside came up with Harmon in tow.

Kyle grinned. "But of course—if I packed up an' went home an' Haggerty had to beat the story outa Harmon, here, he'd have to get the credit, wouldn't he?"

"Anything you say, Sheriff," Mike said.

Kyle put his gun aside and walked confidently to the door. "You'll fix that up in the papers, huh?" he said to Mike.

He walked on and Haggerty made no move to stop him.

They Killed Him Dead

Chapter One

WHEN you see a man standing with a smoking revolver in his hand, staring in sudden terror at a crumpled body, and when you see all this happen, then almost any man would say that it was murder—or at least a killing.

"Careful" Cassidy, rounding a corner an instant after the shot slapped sharply through the murky street, considered it as such. The man who held the pistol was beginning to relax, slowly, sagging with the realization of what he had done. He still stared at the dead one.

Careful Cassidy strode up and gently took the revolver from the killer's hand. He met no protest whatever. The light in the center of the street, striking the man's face, showed a thin mouth and thin nostrils which quivered slightly.

"I've . . . I've killed him," gasped the man.

Careful Cassidy took out a pair of shining bracelets and deftly snapped them to the man's wrists. Then he knelt professionally over the crumpled heap of dirty clothing and felt for a heartbeat. That unsuccessfully done, Cassidy turned the body over and inspected the wound, which was dead center between the man's eyes.

"Stick around," said Cassidy to the killer. "I'm Cassidy

21

from the homicide squad, and you couldn't have picked a neater minute for the job, and you couldn't have done it better."

For the first time the killer seemed to realize that another man was there. He stared down at his confined wrists and then back at Cassidy. For a moment he must have considered running away, for he stared with some hope up and down the deserted, shabby street.

But Cassidy was tough. Cassidy wore a bowler and a cigar and unpressed pants. He wasn't very tall, but he had a square face which scowled eternally even in his happiest moments, and he had a set to his shoulders which showed determination.

The killer did not run.

"He . . . he attacked me!" cried the man. "I came around that corner and he lunged straight at me from behind that lamppost. He was trying to kill me, I tell you."

"You knew him, of course?" said Cassidy.

The killer stared intently at the gray, unshaven face of the dead man, noted the worn condition of the clothes and the curiously rigid shoes, and then shook his head.

"No, I didn't know him."

"He looks like a mob gunner," ventured Cassidy, "but that don't mean anything, of course. Supposing you step into this drugstore with me, and let me call in the wagon."

Cassidy herded his captive into the store and called headquarters. When he came out again he noticed, with some annoyance, that a crowd had begun to gather. He held them back from the corpse and waited.

Soon sirens came and bluecoats unloaded themselves and loaded the stiff and the killer.

22

"Open and shut," Cassidy told the sergeant.

The sergeant looked at him, remembered Cassidy's reputation, and said, "If you say so, it must be so. Did you see it done?"

"Not exactly, but I almost saw the stiff fall. Let's go, boys."

They went. When they got back to headquarters, Cassidy sent for the coroner. He was confident of his procedure. It wasn't usual to leave a stiff lying around on the street and the case, as he had said, was open and shut, and that was all there was to it.

All he had to establish now was the motive, if it had been a killing of spite. To that end he sat down across from the killer and began to fire questions, very careful questions, which showed that Cassidy knew all about his business.

"I tell you," wailed the killer finally, "I didn't even see him there. He just jumped out at me and started to fight, and he had a gun in his hand, and it fell down and I picked it up, and then he tackled me again and I gave it to him.

"My name, Officer, is Smith. I'm not the kind of fellow that goes around bumping guys off just for the fun of it. I never saw him before and all I know is that I had to shoot him to keep him from shooting me.

"I'm a bookkeeper by trade, and I don't have anything to do with gangs or anything. He just jumped me and I had to shoot him."

"Hmm," said Careful Cassidy, elevating his cigar to a firing angle and looking very careful and wise. "It looks kind of funny to me. But investigation will bring it all out. Yes, I'm sure it will."

He saw that Smith was securely locked in a cell and then went down the corridor, saying "Humph" at every third step, and scowling hard as though deep in thought. He met the coroner outside and favored that dapper man, who stood twirling his pince-nez upon its black cord, with a scowl deeper than the other's.

"I say, Cassidy—" began the coroner.

"Tut-tut, Brant, tut-tut, don't give me any of your foolish theories. I know what I'm doing, and I wouldn't do anything which wasn't right. After all, I've got to think of my reputation. That man says his name is Smith. They all say that. He says he's a bookkeeper and that must be a lie, too. He says the man attacked him, and that he shot the guy with the guy's own gun, but that's a lie, too."

"But, Cassidy—"

"But me no buts, Brant. You don't know about these things, and there isn't much use in your butting into this. Stay with your stiffs, and leave me the live ones. My reputation is too good to be questioned on this matter. Didn't I practically see it happen?"

"Yes, yes, but—"

"Well, dammit, out with it," snorted Cassidy.

"The fact is, Cassidy, that this man was not killed with a gun. He was stabbed to death with a knife," said the coroner.

Careful Cassidy had reason to blink. He saw then that he had been careless in spite of everything. He should have looked very carefully about the street for other weapons. But then, dammit, he had, hadn't he? He had everything down in his report and everything ready for the investigation, and now Brant said . . .

"What was that again?" pleaded Cassidy.

"I said that the fellow was killed with a knife. Stabbed three times in the back, each of the wounds fatal. As soon as I get down to the morgue I'll have an autopsy made and we'll know exactly how long he's been dead."

Brant was beaming, twirling his glasses, and looking most pleased with himself. Although Cassidy did not know it, there were many men about the station and the city who would very much have liked to see him make just one mistake. Cassidy's record was far too perfect, his luck was much too good—as was attested this night by Fates letting him step right on to the scene of the crime.

"What time did you see this happen?" said Brant.

"Nine-thirteen," said Careful Cassidy. "Listen, are you sure about those knife wounds? I mean mightn't they have—"

"I'm certain," said Brant. "And the wounds are rather old—say a couple of hours, at a guess. He was dead before he was shot."

"But, dammit," scowled Cassidy, "this guy Smith said that the fellow attacked him, and if that's the case, then . . . then . . . lord, but the guy must have been dead at the time!"

Cassidy stomped back for a look at the stiff, which was about to be removed. He saw that the coroner was right. Three knife wounds, deep and fatal knife wounds, any one of which would have done the job, were very apparent in the man's back.

Cassidy was so agitated by this discovery that he merely flipped through the papers found on the dead man. The fellow was probably some petty thief, from the looks of his loot, but Cassidy could not find further identifying clue.

"Hm, hmm, hmmm," scowled Cassidy. "I get the Parsons' killer dead to rights. I get the Sanderson case open and shut. I get those dead bankers all solved. I even turn the juice into the governor's killer. And now," he groaned, "and now I have to take a beating from some dumb hood nobody either knows or cares about!"

With wrath at such a state of affairs bubbling and seething like a cauldron of poison in his vitals, he decided that he had better go back to the scene of the crime. He did not miss Brant's knowing look as he went out. They were laughing at him.

Chapter Two

ONCE again he found the dirty street. At the earlier hour he had been on his way to Mike's Palace for a glass of cold beer before bed, but now Mike was forgotten. Cassidy paused upon the corner and looked intently down at the spot where the dead man had lain.

When his first scrutiny disclosed nothing, he took out his flashlight and began to explore the street on his hands and knees. Rooney, fat and big and jolly, walking his beat, came by and stood rocking back and forth on the curb, watching Cassidy's antics. Cassidy heard the patrolman's laugh and flushed. He did not reply to Rooney's question. A sudden discovery made him forget all about Rooney.

He had found a trail of blood which led straight down the sidewalk. True, it wasn't very much blood, only a little drop about every five feet or so, but the flashlight picked them out, and Cassidy followed them in a crouch like some bloodhound upon the trail of an escaped convict.

The drops led up a flight of steps and Cassidy, upon inspection, discovered that he was at the side door of a Greek restaurant. The place looked to be of somewhat evil reputation, if a quantity of dirt and the smell of decaying slops were any indication.

Cassidy entered, and saw that there were no patrons.

Only the owner stood guard, wiping his hands nervously upon a dirty apron and staring at Cassidy out of sucked-in eyes which appeared to be carefully packed in larded cotton.

"You . . . you want something to eat?" he questioned.

"Naw," said Cassidy, scowling like a storm cloud. "I'm Cassidy from the homicide squad."

The Greek began to shake. He dropped his apron and began to twist at his mustache.

"But . . . but why do you come here? I know nothing about it. I don't know who . . ."

He knew then that he was giving himself away. Cassidy went across the room and took the Greek's arm. Cassidy was scowling terribly, until it looked as though his face would explode and spatter the room with screaming fragments.

Carefully, Cassidy began to lead the man toward the stairs. The Greek went willingly enough, so Cassidy changed his direction. He went toward the kitchen, and the Greek recoiled as though Cassidy had faced him with a ghost.

Relentlessly, Cassidy led on. The Greek pulled back harder and harder. Cassidy stopped and the Greek relaxed. Cassidy started again, and the Greek drew back.

It was a silent battle, without any great effort. It was merely a mind reader's trick, getting a dupe to lead the way to a hidden object. The process led Cassidy out the rear door and into a court which looked like a cube of solidified coal smoke, hemmed in by eight-foot gray walls.

Now the Greek began to blubber and Cassidy scowled in triumph.

"So this is where you did it?" said Cassidy, prowling about the place and snooping into the corners with his flashlight.

The Greek stood in silent palsy, kneading his pudgy fingers, and when Cassidy spotted a patch of blood, he could stand it no longer. He cracked with a sound like a bursting paper bag.

"I had to do it!" yowled the Greek. "I had to do it! I don't try to cover anything up, and it ain't no crime to stay alive like I did!"

Cassidy poked methodically through the trash and finally unearthed a lethal-looking butcher knife, which he handled delicately, his handkerchief protecting any possible prints.

"Now talk!" he snarled.

"Oh, oh, oh, I knew there was nothing good coming of this. I knew it. Listen to me. Two nights now some feller has been sneaking over the back of that wall stealing things from me. So tonight I'm here cleaning me some rabbits, and this feller jumps right on top of my neck.

"He was six, seven, maybe eight feet tall, and he had a gun, and he yelled, 'I'm going to kill you,' and then he was all over me. And what could I do? I got this knife, and so I stab him."

"A likely story," muttered Cassidy. "Humph!"

He called a wagon on the Greek's phone, and soon the patrol arrived in the Black Maria, and the Greek was loaded in. But this time Cassidy was more careful than before. He examined the spikes on top of the wall and found a piece of torn cloth the same color as the dead man's coat. This he took, waving it like a battle flag, and sat himself down beside the Greek in the wagon.

Back at headquarters, he saw that the Greek was locked up for further investigation. He did not believe the man's story in full, although the piece of cloth seemed to mean something. But he had at least made some attempt to solve this crime in a proper, careful fashion. Now he had the killer, and that was that.

He went down to the morgue, and was startled to see that Brant was still there. Brant had a cat-and-cream expression on his face, but Cassidy disregarded that.

Somewhat loftily, Cassidy said, "I got it now. A Greek killed him in back of a restaurant. I never fail, Brant, and that's saying more than you can for coroners. Uh-huh, this cloth matches and that's that. The Greek killed him, and we'll find out the real story behind it in the morning."

Brant, in his white apron, still swung his glasses on their black cord. "By the way, Cassidy, I might venture to say that—" he began.

"Tut-tut, Brant, nothing more to say about it. Don't crow over it. Someday you'll regret it. That wasn't a mistake of mine, that was a mere oversight, and I would have seen it myself if you hadn't—"

"But the corpse—" began Brant, patiently and sarcastically.

"Damn the corpse!" cried Cassidy in terrible disrespect. "What's wrong with the corpse now?"

"The time of death was about six o'clock," said Brant. "About six o'clock. And the knife wounds—"

"What's the matter with the knife wounds? I thought they were fatal, and now I suppose you are going to tell me that he died from water on the kneecap or something."

30

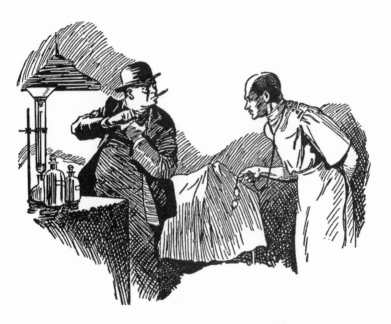

*"Damn the corpse!" cried Cassidy in terrible disrespect.
"What's wrong with the corpse now?"*

"Not quite, old fellow, not quite. You see, the fact is"—Brant stopped and flavored his words with honey—"the fact is, my dear fellow, that the knife wounds were not fatal, could not have been fatal, because—"

Cassidy felt the sweat starting out of him, and the cigar he chewed drooped. "Go on, dammit!"

"—because he died from a broken spine and internal injuries."

Cassidy jumped as though stung. "Go on, this isn't funny. What do you think I am? A school kid, to believe all that? Spine, my hat! I got the man who did it and that's all there is to it."

"No use to bluster, Cassidy. No use at all," said Brant sweetly. "I have just now discovered that four vertebrae are smashed and that the back was terribly bruised. The blood from the knife wounds was not active and flowing. Perhaps it might have dripped a little, but the age of the wounds show that they were made on a corpse, not a live man. You see, such a wound would bruise, and in this case there is no bruise about the knife wounds. You can't bruise a corpse, old chap. The spine was broken in a long fall somewhere about an hour before the knife wounds were inserted."

Cassidy heard Brant laughing behind him. And, in another's shoes, he would have laughed himself. Indeed, the thing was funny when you came to think of it. . . . Impossible, too. But the coroner was always right and . . .

"The question is," said Cassidy to himself, drooping and feeling slightly ill and that somebody was making a fool of him, "the question is, where did the guy get his busted spine?"

He took himself back to the restaurant and found that the Greek's wife had taken over. He had nothing to say to her, although she had plenty to say to him in a high, shrill voice which cut like the Greek's butcher knife.

Cassidy stumped about the court, pulled up a box and again examined the stone wall. But he could find nothing there except that this court was backed by another court.

He thought that over. To get into the Greek's backyard a man would have to go through the house beyond the other court. Therefore, reasoning simply, the dead man must have come out of that house.

Cassidy dropped over into the other yard. He was feeling tough again, and he paused to light a new cigar. He set his hat at a frightening angle and thundered upon the basement door.

After a long wait, a face peered timidly at him. Cassidy elbowed his way into the room.

"I'm Cassidy of the homicide squad. Who are you?"

"I-I-I am the janitor and . . ." The small, white-faced man looked very nervous. He was bent over from work, and his face bore heavy lines of worry. His eyes were all washed out. He looked like some castoff winter coat grown too threadbare for use.

"Hm, hmm, hmmm," said Cassidy, with his best scowl. "What's the matter with you?"

"A slight chill. I stayed out too late last night and . . . But maybe you want to see the doctor?"

"And where is the doctor?" barked Cassidy.

The janitor led the way up a long flight of back stairs. They came out upon a dingy landing. By the light of a small yellow bulb they could read "Doctor" upon the door at the head of the front stairs.

The janitor's nervousness was increasing, much to Cassidy's satisfaction. The janitor knocked. Presently a tired-looking woman came and told them that the doctor had been out all afternoon and would not be back until late. "But you can wait there on that bench if you want to."

Cassidy wasn't interested in benches. He was interested in the janitor. Cassidy prided himself upon his remarkable luck.

As soon as the woman was gone, Cassidy confronted the man.

"Why," said Cassidy in a voice which shook the flimsy walls, "why did you do it?"

A shot in the dark, thought Cassidy behind his scowl. The janitor cringed and looked involuntarily down the front steps.

Chapter Three

CASSIDY also looked. He saw that the railing at the bottom had recently been patched. He went down there and saw that the glue was still wet. He also noted that the carpet tacks were ripped out in two places on the stairs. It was very plain to him then.

"Come clean," said Cassidy to the janitor. "I've got the goods, and you better tell me all about it, and fast." The flash of a shield and the scowl did the trick. The janitor wilted.

"I tell you," whined the man, all bent over with woe, "that it was all an accident. I came up here to clean up, and when I went down again I passed this landing, and a man was sitting on the bench. I . . . I tripped on him and he suddenly jumped up and grabbed me and tried to throw me down. But I fought him off and . . . and when I did he . . . he stumbled and fell all the way down. When . . . when I got down there he was dead."

"A likely story!" sneered Cassidy. "You murdered him, and I'm going to find out why in the morning. You haven't got strength enough to shove a big guy like he was down those stairs if he didn't want to go. You're under arrest, so come along quietly."

Without further questions and with great determination, Cassidy dropped his nickel into the pay phone in the hall and called the wagon.

"Say," said the desk sergeant, "do you think we got nothing to do but grab up your killers?" There was a slight laugh in his voice, and Cassidy took it ill and began to say things. But the sergeant hung up, and soon the patrol wagon came.

Cassidy saw to it that the janitor was locked securely in his cell. Cassidy was beginning to get a little bit worried about the way he was filling up the jail, but then the occasion seemed to demand such a thing. There was something ominous behind all this and in the morning . . .

Brant came out of an inner office. He had been waiting, although the hour was late. Brant was smiling again, and Cassidy almost bashed him one.

"By the way, Cassidy," drawled Brant, "you know that man you saw shot this evening?"

"Can it!" cried Cassidy in agony. He knew what was coming. He could hear them snickering in the squad room. Careful Cassidy was making an ass of himself, and he knew it.

"Well, I'm sorry about my misinformation, Cassidy," continued Brant. "I should have made a more thorough investigation beforehand, but you've been so impetuous that—"

"Dammit!" screamed Cassidy. "I have not! I've been acting on information you gave me and . . ." Words failed him. He knew what was coming.

"I was somewhat astonished," said Brant, "when I found that there were no bruises to mention, in spite of that spine trouble, and so I went to work and took the whole cadaver apart, and I found—"

Cassidy moaned, "What did you find?"

Brant drew out a dinner ring. It was a cheap affair, set with small gaudy stones. It was big and sharp and green. Brant let it sparkle in the light.

"This," said Brant, "was in his throat."

"In his throat?"

"Yes, I'm sorry to say that this was the cause of death. He swallowed this ring, choked on it, and then died when it lodged across his windpipe."

"This is a joke," pleaded Cassidy.

"No, I assure you it is not. I found this ring only when I discovered that his blood had rushed to his head, and that he had collapsed lungs. Then I looked for the ring and here it is."

Cassidy staggered out of there. He went to his desk and found that he had carefully saved the papers and the small items he had taken from the dead man.

He found, among them, two other rings of the same size as the emerald-colored one. He found, also, a wallet with a dollar bill in it. This wallet looked as though it had come from a bigger pocketbook, perhaps a woman's, in that the wallet smelled of face powder and perfume. It contained a driver's license which bore the name "Emma Lindsay," and the address of 224 Spring Street.

Cassidy was haggard. They were still snickering in the squad room. Careful Cassidy's reputation was slowly going up in smoke. And it had to be over a bum nobody cared about at all. Why the hell had he ever come onto the scene in the first place?

It was getting late, and Cassidy decided that he had better

take a taxi. He wanted none of the patrol cars because he knew that the radio cops would laugh at him all the way.

He went back into the murky night and rode sullenly to 224 Spring Street. He had the wallet in his hand when he rang the bell.

A beefy, red-faced and overbearing man answered the door. His whole attitude was a threat, and he seemed about to demand that Cassidy take himself elsewhere at such an ungodly hour. But Cassidy, cigar tilted up and feeling better already, beat him to the draw. Cassidy shoved the pocketbook under his nose.

"I believe this belonged to Mrs. Lindsay," said Cassidy.

The man's eyes protruded as though pushed out by terrific mental pressure. He fell back from the door and Cassidy took that as permission to enter. A woman was standing in the hall, staring at him. She was as timid as her husband was overbearing. She was dressed in house clothes which were somewhat gaudy. She was the kind who hopes to hide a timorous heart by a loud exterior.

"I brought you back this wallet," said Cassidy. "I'm Cassidy of the homicide squad."

She took the purse as though it were hot. Her husband still held open the door. But Cassidy did not take the hint. Cassidy drew the dinner ring out of his pocket and held it out.

With a small gasp, she seized upon it and then, as though afraid to leave it lying about, slipped it quickly upon her finger. It fitted perfectly.

"That's fine," said Cassidy, beginning to scowl. He drew

the dead man's gun from his pocket and shoved it at the man. "Ever see this before?"

"No!" shouted the man. "No!"

"That's fine," said Cassidy. "Then it's your gun, perhaps?"

The woman began to weep. She clutched at her husband's arm and moaned, "We've done nothing wrong. We didn't mean to—"

"That's all I wanted to know," said Cassidy. "So you did kill him? Oh, there's no use putting on an act for me. I know all about it. *All* about it. You're coming down to the station house with me for questioning."

"No, wait!" thundered Lindsay. "I'll tell you all about it. There's no use in your . . ."

But Cassidy already had the wagon on the phone, and he ignored the gibes which came back to him through the earpiece.

The driver saw it was Cassidy when he arrived. He chuckled. The driver had a perfect right to laugh, but Cassidy's scowl was horrible to behold.

"Still the same corpse?" said the driver.

Cassidy didn't answer that and they safely arrived at headquarters.

Brant was still there, grinning. Cassidy planted himself and his cigar belligerently before the coroner.

"You find that he was poisoned yet?" demanded Cassidy.

"No, he choked to death," said Brant.

"I'll bet it was poison," said Cassidy. "Sergeant, get these people out here. I want to do some questioning."

Smith, the bookkeeper, came, followed by the shivering Greek, who in turn was followed by the janitor. All three of them stood nervously in the bullpen waiting for Cassidy to start.

"Now," said Cassidy, turning to Lindsay and his wife. "What happened? And tell it straight or . . ."

Lindsay began to talk in a heavy voice, but his wife interrupted him.

"I was in the kitchen," said the woman, "and this man came around to the back door and asked me if I had something to eat. He was a big, tough-looking man, and I thought I'd better do what he said, and so I started to get him something.

"He came in and sat down, and grumbled when I said all I had was some bread and butter and milk. He said I'd better have more than that or he'd fix me.

"It was about six o'clock, and I thought my husband would be home any minute, but he didn't come right then, and this man kept getting uglier and uglier, and I saw I couldn't hold him off anymore.

"My pocketbook and my rings, that I'd taken off to get supper, were lying on the shelf, but I didn't think much about it. I was worried because this man looked so tough and talked so horribly.

"I made some excuse and went out into the other room, intending to phone for the police, but I met my husband coming in.

"I told him and right away he got his revolver out of the desk and with an awful yell he charged out into the kitchen, to drive this man out of the house.

40

"The man must have heard him coming, because when I got there I saw that the man was standing with his hands over his head, and my husband told me to search him and make sure he hadn't stolen anything out of the place.

"Then all of a sudden the man turned red and blue in the face and began to cough and doubled up on the floor and writhed something awful.

"So my husband got scared. He thought maybe we better not call the police, as that would mean a lot of unpleasant publicity, and we couldn't stand that, and so I said we'd better take him around the corner to the doctor's as fast as possible.

"The man was still alive when we got there, we thought, but all of a sudden I realized he was dead, and Herman—that's my husband—he said we'd better not have any dead man with us, so we put him on the bench at the top of the steps and ran away. Nobody heard us or saw us."

"Uh-huh," said Cassidy, scowling and gnawing on his cigar. "Just as I thought. He must have stuck your ring in his mouth to hide it, and then choked on it. And now you," he said, turning to the janitor.

"Honest, it was just like I said," quavered the old man. "Except I thought . . . I guess I made it sound kind of wild because I just touched him, and down the steps he went.

"And then, being scared on account of thinking I killed him, I carried him out to the back myself before anybody saw him and dumped him over the garden wall into the next court."

Cassidy's scowl was most terrible to behold, and the janitor folded into himself like an accordion.

Cassidy's glare passed on to the Greek and the Greek, who

41

had been fully prepared for this onslaught, immediately lost all his wits. He stammered and kneaded his pudgy fingers and shuffled his feet.

"Come on," snarled Cassidy. "Out with it. Just what did you do?"

The Greek whimpered, "I didn't mean any harm. It was just like I said. I was so scared I raised my knife when he hit my back, and I let him have it. I saw his gun—honest, I saw it—and I thought he was going to shoot me."

"How about that gun?" thundered Cassidy.

Lindsay averted his gaze. "I thought maybe it would look bad if I had a gun in the house, so I put it in his pocket."

"Hm," said Cassidy. "Hm, hmm, hmmm. Go on."

The Greek marshalled his courage again and said, "I knew if I called the police, then my business might maybe be ruined, and so I thought maybe it would be best, perhaps, if I took him down the block and stood him up against a lamppost. I shoved his gun back into his pocket, but his coat was torn and it wouldn't stay. And then I beat it."

"And you?" cried Cassidy to the bookkeeper.

"Honest, I didn't mean nothing. But a couple fellers that I owed money to said they'd get me, and I touched this guy when I came around the corner, and he sort of slumped at me—I guess he sort of slumped. I thought he jumped. Honest, I thought he did. And so I socked him in the jaw and the gun clattered, and he kept leaning into me and I kept slugging him and finally he almost had me down, and there was the gun, so I shot him."

Cassidy patrolled the bullpen for five minutes. Five sets

of eyes followed him anxiously. Finally Cassidy came to a decision in the case. He couldn't hold five people for one death, and you couldn't hold a man for defending his own house, especially when the dead man had actually committed a sort of suicide.

They would all have to explain themselves later, but the judge would let them off. Cassidy himself couldn't see any crime except their failure to call in the police, and that was small enough.

Careful Cassidy had solved it at last. He uptilted his cigar, adjusted his bowler, and for once he smiled—because, after all, the situation was funny.

"Go on home, you people. Go on, clear out!" he ordered.

They went, talking excitedly among themselves, immensely relieved.

In the squad room, Cassidy told them the story. Brant was still there, and Brant laughed hardest of all. Careful Cassidy beamed. They weren't laughing at him; they were laughing with him.

"For a while," said Careful Cassidy, "it looked like I'd have to arrest every man in town. Lucky I came along when I did, or I would have had to, I guess."

The Mad Dog Murder

The Mad Dog Murder

TOMMY FARRELL awoke with a start and gave an attentive ear to the police announcer's voice which rasped out of the squad car speaker.

"Car Seventeen. Calling Car Seventeen. Proceed to fifteen Belmont Street. Fifteen Belmont Street. A mad dog reported."

Tommy Farrell gave Butch Hanlon a meaning glance and Butch Hanlon shivered.

"Damned cold weather for mad dogs," said Farrell, throwing the car in gear and shooting on the siren.

"Aw, they get mad any time," said Butch, from the depths of his blue overcoat collar.

The squad car took the icy streets like a charge of light cavalry. The deserted city was not dangerous at this time of morning, but the noise of the siren and the speed made Farrell warm.

"Still, I don't think mad dogs are usual," insisted Farrell, knocking a garbage can from the curb with a wild skid.

Butch Hanlon watched the white street straighten out before them and then, screwing up his head and getting his mouth in sight, he said, "You're always suspicious of everything. One of these days you'll land on the homicide

47

squad and you better start your investigations then. Don't forget, Tommy lad, you're still a patrolman on wheels."

"Yeah? Well, one of these days I'll get my break and you'll be saying yessir to me and walking soft. I'm not going to be a perambulating flatfoot forever."

"You won't be anything if you don't slow down. What's the hurry? Bored with life or something? I got a wife and kid waiting for me."

"Keep your shirt on, copper, here we are."

The car skidded to a stop before a large apartment house and unloaded its two occupants. Tommy Farrell loomed over Butch Hanlon like Goliath over David. Tommy Farrell was wide-shouldered and handsome-faced, dark, and very good to look at. Butch was so ugly he was almost handsome himself.

They clumped into the welcomely warm foyer and leaned over the desk.

"Okay, we're here," said Farrell. "Where's the mad dog?"

The girl looked up in surprise. "Mad dog?"

"Yeah, didn't somebody call out of here about a mad dog?"

"Why, no." She looked from one trooper to the other and her black eyes were wide with questioning. If Farrell had not been so preoccupied with the case he might have noticed that she was the most beautiful woman he had ever seen.

She was saved from further investigation by the appearance of a white-haired, frock-coated man of very respectable appearance.

"Ah, there you are," said this man. "I've been phoning and phoning and—"

"Lead away," said Farrell. "Where's the mad dog?"

"He was running through the halls and he darted into poor Mr. Meyers' rooms. I heard a shriek and—"

"How long ago was this?" snapped Farrell. "Lead off, you fool. Maybe it's bit somebody by this time."

The switchboard girl stared after them, suddenly troubled. The handkerchief she held in her hands went into two tiny pieces.

Farrell was out of the elevator first. The man in the frock coat pointed toward a nearby door. Both Farrell and Butch could hear the whines and the moans coming out of that room. Fearing the worst, they tried the knob.

"Locked," said Butch.

"You gotta key?" said Farrell.

"Why, no, Mr. Meyers—"

"One, two—" said Butch.

"Three!" cried Farrell.

The door splintered away from its lock and slammed down to the floor. Farrell's first impression was that a brown muff had been rolled across the rug and that a black sheet was tossing on the couch.

The dog, a Pekingese, darted under an overstuffed chair and stayed there, whimpering in fright. The man, a fellow with gray hair and a pain-twisted, ancient face, was twitching across the room.

The man in the frock coat drew back in fear. "There he is! Shoot him! Shoot him!"

Involuntarily, Farrell's right hand stabbed toward his holster, but the gun never appeared. "Hell, it's just a pup."

"There he is! Shoot him! Shoot him!"

He paid the dog no further attention, but went immediately toward the couch.

Mr. Meyers was jibbering. His left hand showed a ragged set of teeth marks which were already puffy. Blood flowed from a slight scalp wound. But the man's worst injury was stark fright.

Farrell gave Butch a meaning glance, already feeling that everyone was being a little too dramatic. A man in a skullcap thrust his head through the doorway and hugged his nightgown close about him. This fellow was to the front of several residents who had been routed out by the noise.

Suddenly the Pekingese decided to make a run for it. Staggering and bleary-eyed, panting with exhaustion, the animal spurted for the door.

Not until then did Farrell see the foam. "Good God, he *is* mad!"

"Shoot him!" howled the people, scrambling back from the door.

Butch flipped out his Colt but Farrell struck it aside. The Peke turned away from the excitement before him and with tongue lolling from foam-flecked lips, dived for Farrell's legs.

Farrell had his coat off in an instant. He threw it over the brown bit of fluff and, protecting his own hands, tucked the dog under his arm.

The man in the frock coat bellowed, "He'll bite you!"

The man in the skullcap merely gaped.

People came crowding back into the apartment to stare at Meyers.

"Listen, Butch," said Farrell, "phone for an ambulance right away and get Meyers to a hospital. And take this dog—"

"Nawsir," said Butch stolidly. "I gotta wife and kid, I have. You take the dog."

"All right, but get the ambulance." And when Butch disappeared, Farrell turned to the man in the frock coat. "What's your name?"

"Me . . . Oh, I'm Thomas Harrison. I own this building."

"Then how come you didn't have a passkey?"

"Mr. Meyers wouldn't allow it."

"Huh, that's funny. Then can you tell me who owns this dog?"

The man looked sideways and down toward the elevator, unwilling to answer the question.

Farrell turned to the man in the skullcap. "Who are you?"

"I'm Dr. Murphy, Officer. I've got my office here in this building. I was about to remark that you had better get Meyers treatment right away. That dog is obviously mad. The stagger and the expression and the foam—"

"Got a laboratory, huh?" said Farrell.

"Why, yes."

"I see," said Farrell, slowly.

The men in the doorway moved aside to allow the switchboard girl to enter. She came with flushed face and shaking hands, staring at the bundle Farrell held in his arms.

"Did you . . . did you . . ."

"Did I what? Say, is this your dog I've got here?"

At that moment a pink tongue tipped by a black nose projected through an opening in the coat. The people in the room cried out a warning, and Farrell tucked the nose and tongue back in.

"Toto," cried the girl. "Oh, I thought he'd . . . give him to me."

52

"No, ma'am. He's mad."

"But he's my dog and there isn't a thing wrong with him."

"No, he bit Meyers and . . ."

Fear flashed over the girl's face, and then anger. "Give him to me, I tell you. You can't have him."

Farrell was spared a scene by the arrival of the ambulance.

An intern, shivering in his whites, said, "Looks like it's all right. Come along, Tony."

Farrell started to follow them out, but the girl caught his arm. "Look here, Officer, that's my dog and you can't have him. I'm . . ."

Farrell, with regret, shook himself free and went down the stairs. Behind him the girl was crying. Farrell went faster and slammed the door behind him.

Instead of reporting straight to the precinct, Farrell routed out the coroner and confronted that worthy in his living room.

"This is a helluva time to—" began the coroner.

"No, listen, Hardy," said Farrell. "Do me a favor, will you? I been trying like the devil to get appointed to the homicide squad. You know that. Well, you can do me a big favor, if you want."

"What you got under your arm?" said Hardy, beetling through horn-rimmed glasses.

"It's a dog. A Pekingese named Toto. I—"

"What do you think I am? A vet? Take your dog and—"

"No, wait a minute," pleaded Farrell. "This dog is supposed to be mad."

Hardy jumped back and threw up his hands as Farrell made to loose the dog.

Butch came in then and called Farrell off. "Aw, come on, let's take him down to the gas chamber at the pound. You ain't going to get anyplace with that. He's nuts, Doc. Ever since he got the idea he wanted to get on the homicide squad he tries to make a murder out of everything. The other night he was positively droolin' when we found a body in the gutter by the wharves, and then we found that the guy was only drunk. The only killing around here is goin' to be me from his drivin'."

"No, listen," wheedled Farrell. "I got a hot idea. I want—"

"Take it to the pound and let them gas it," said Hardy.

"That won't prove anything," argued Farrell. "I got to find out if this dog is really mad. You got all the stuff here and you're crazy on the subject of investigation. Now, if there's something to this . . ."

Hardy gave up gracefully. "All right, there's a drygoods box out back. Put the pooch in it and I'll see what I can do when the hour's a little more reasonable."

Farrell deposited his burden in the box. The Pekingese was terribly sick, its eyes bulging. Farrell argued Hardy into doing something for the animal then.

But all the Peke wanted was a drink and when this had been given, it curled up in a corner and went to sleep. Hardy took some of the froth from the lips and went into his laboratory. Farrell and Butch went back to the precinct to go off duty.

"Don't say anything about what we did with the dog," said Farrell. "And don't tell them what I think."

"Think I want to be laughed off the force?" said Butch, cynically.

For several days routine went on as usual. The only interruption came when Farrell dropped back to see the girl at the switchboard. He found that her name was June Beach and that she was far prettier than he had first imagined.

"Your dog's with a friend of mine," said Farrell. "He's being treated all right and maybe I can bring him back to you in first-rate condition."

"I hope so. I . . . I haven't got so many friends, Mr. Farrell, and Toto was kind of understanding. Mr. Harrison, the owner, let me keep him as a special favor. You see, Doctor Murphy keeps a lot of animals in the building, guinea pigs and such, and I argued that—"

"What's he keep them for?"

"Oh, experiments. You ought to smell the top floor sometime. But the doctor pays his rent regularly and so Harrison didn't mind. . . ."

"What is this guy Murphy?"

"A bacteriologist and toxicologist. He's a funny fellow. I can't see how he gets any pleasure out of making little pigs and monkeys suffer from all kinds of diseases."

"Uh-huh," said Farrell, very interested.

And all that night Butch Hanlon found Farrell a bad companion. Contrary to his usual way, Farrell had nothing at all to say. Farrell was doing some tall dreaming.

He saw himself a plainclothesman with a detective shield, drawing a salary two can live upon, and he saw himself coming home to a flat and to June, and to maybe a couple kids who would grow up to be big cops and . . .

The next morning he was so elated he had to see June Beach again. She was taking an early trick at the switchboard, and he knew that he shouldn't bother her at work, but she saw him come in and she took off her earphones.

"Mr. Farrell," she called. And when he was closer, she said, "Mr. Farrell, I'm so worried about my uncle. I tried to get in touch with him at the hospital last night. . . ."

"Your uncle?" said Farrell, astounded.

"Why, yes. Didn't you know Meyers was my uncle?"

"But he had a fine apartment and—"

"I know. It does seem odd. But I didn't want him to keep me, and I tried to make my own way, but he's a very suspicious man. He wouldn't let me get a job out of his sight, and so I got this one here."

"Listen," said Farrell, "if you lived in that apartment, then Toto liked your uncle, didn't he?"

At the mention of the dog she turned a shade whiter and sank down at the switchboard. She didn't look straight at Farrell again. He had too many duties on his hands to linger.

At the first pay station he called the hospital.

"This is the Police Department," said Farrell in an authoritative voice. "I want to know the condition of a Mr. Meyers who was brought to you with a bitten hand."

"He is very low," said the hospital clerk. "He is not expected to live more than an hour or two."

Farrell went straight to the hospital and blustered his way into Meyers' room. The sight which met his eyes was not pleasant. Meyers was no longer vicious, but the straps still held him down. Meyers was the color of the bedsheet and his jaw muscles were tight.

After fifteen minutes, Farrell and the doctor went out into the hall. The doctor was marking up a death certificate.

"Very easily diagnosed," said the doctor. "No question about it at all. Rabies, received from dog bite. I would have had his niece brought here to see him toward the end, but the man was in no condition to be seen. The shock would have prostrated the girl. By the way, Officer, has the dog that bit him been killed?"

Farrell saw fit to pass that up. "Listen, Doc, isn't it funny for a dog to go mad in the middle of winter? I thought—"

"That hasn't anything to do with it. He was somehow exposed to the disease and— By the way, you'd better have your men check this. We don't want any rabies epidemic filling up our wards."

Farrell went out with leaden feet. He stopped outside the hospital and lit a cigarette, looking at the big snowflakes which floated down to the street.

Only one course was open to him. He had to report this thing immediately and report what he knew about it. To hold the information would court his own dismissal.

He found the homicide squad lieutenant in his office and went quickly to the point.

"A guy named Meyers just died of rabies up at the hospital," said Farrell.

The big, thick-faced lieutenant swiveled around in his chair. "So what? Anything unusual about it?"

"No, but I think you'd better investigate. I was in there when he got bitten and I took the dog away. It's kind of funny and I thought maybe you'd better look into it."

"No case for me," said the lieutenant, "but maybe I better. Want to come along?"

"No," said Farrell. "I'll wait here."

The lieutenant came back in three hours and shook the snow out of his overcoat. He scowled at Farrell.

"Wild-goose chase, copper."

"What did you find?" pleaded Farrell.

"A gink named Murphy's got a lot of sick pigs and monkeys on the top floor. He's been experimenting on rabies serum and a couple of the monks have got it. The mutt merely ran into the monk, got bitten, went mad and attacked the old man. That's all. Nobody to blame, but I sure gave that dame hell for not watching her dog closer. By the way, Farrell, where's the dog?"

Farrell gulped. Sentiment is one thing and duty is another. He tightened up his face. "Hardy's been holding him."

"Hardy? Since when did the doc become a vet?" The lieutenant smiled and reached for the phone. He contacted Hardy after two calls. "Hello there, what's this I hear about you taking in stray pups? . . . Yeah, the guy died a while ago. Send the dog over to the pound. . . . No, I don't care about that. . . . A trace is enough, isn't it? Hell's bells, man, a guy just died from it. Yeah, send him over to the pound and put him out of his misery."

Farrell thought convulsively of June. He knew he couldn't ever face her again. "He says he found . . . ?"

"Sure. He said there was a trace of it in the dog's mouth, but that the dog was evidently just a carrier and didn't get the disease itself."

"That's funny," said Farrell. "The dog had foam on its mouth when I got it."

"Well, maybe a temporary case or something. Can't make mountains out of molehills all the time, son. Sorry."

For the next three days Butch Hanlon's life was a gruesome dream. The streets were still icy and the way Tommy Farrell threw the squad car around brought that well-known phrase time after time to Butch's lips.

"Dammit, I got a wife and a kid!"

But Butch's pleas were unavailing. Farrell's mood was vicious. When they found two men breaking into an apartment one night for purposes of robbery, the two men were turned into the precinct looking like survivors of a train wreck. Farrell's fists were sore and he took a gloating pleasure in their pain.

He rarely had anything to say and Butch became frankly worried about him. But nothing Butch could say helped.

"Aw, come on, Tommy," pleaded Butch. "You'll find a real good murder someday and solve it by yourself and they'll take you on the squad. In the meantime, remember that I got a wife and a kid."

But if Farrell felt bad about the dog, he felt terrible one morning when he was summoned to the lieutenant's office.

"Farrell," said the lieutenant, "I've been following this rabies thing out of curiosity, wondering if something would turn up. It did. I believe you know this young lady." He tossed a rogues' gallery photo across the desk.

Farrell gasped as he recognized June Beach. "But how...?"

"We nailed her," said the lieutenant with satisfaction. "Thanks to your tip we nailed her. I might have let this thing pass if you hadn't brought it to my attention. They've just read Meyers' will."

"His will?"

"Yeah. I've been scouting around and I find out that he's a pretty miserly old guy with plenty of money. About fifty thousand in securities. And he left every nickel of it to this Beach dame. Open-and-shut case."

But Farrell did not want to believe it. "I don't understand."

"She hands rabies to the dog via one monk, gets the dog to bite the old man and kills him. They tell me up there that she and the old guy used to fight something terrible. He wouldn't give her a cent and wouldn't let her go out at all. So, out of spite, she cooks this up. Pretty nervy for a dame, but she confessed when we'd questioned her all night."

"You mean . . . you've got her here now?"

"Why not? Hell, man, don't look so pale. I thought this would be good news for you. Your tip . . ."

But Farrell was already gone. He went down the cold corridors to the cells, and there he found June Beach. She was haggard, sobbing against her arm, but when she saw him she turned defiantly away.

"Listen to me," said Farrell. "Listen, I didn't have anything to do with this, honest. I was just trying—"

"Don't talk to me. First you took my dog, and that didn't satisfy you. Now you've got me in here as a murderer."

"I know you're all in. But why did you confess? You know you didn't do it."

"They . . . they . . ." But no word she could utter could express her horror of that grilling under a glaring light.

"Listen, tell me what you know. I'll work on this. Honest I will. And if I don't succeed, I'll . . . I'll turn in my badge."

Something in his voice made her turn to him, but her nerves were on edge and she could only sob.

He left her after a little and went out to find Butch.

Butch was asleep after his long night in the squad car, but Farrell didn't mind that. "Listen here, we've got to get busy. They've got June Beach behind bars for killing Meyers."

"Well?" said Butch. "You wanted a murder case, didn't you?"

"Oh, my God, man, but not like this."

"Murder's never very nice," said Butch.

"Come on, we're going to the pound."

"What for?"

Farrell didn't answer, he was too worried about what he might find.

But at the pound the attendant led them through the pens to find Toto the Peke sitting alone and forlorn in a small, isolated box. Outside of a great deal of woe, Toto did not appear very sick.

"I didn't have an order," said the attendant. "Hardy just brought him in and dumped him here day before yesterday. I was going to get an order this afternoon. He's a valuable dog and we don't kill them off right away."

"He's supposed to have rabies," said Farrell.

"Him?" said the attendant. "Nuts! I guess I know dogs better than that. It would show up in three days or so."

"I'm taking him along," said Farrell, and proceeded to do so.

Butch shied away from the animal, but when they got in the car, Toto was so glad of human companionship at last that he licked Butch's hand gratefully. Butch grinned and scratched Toto's ear.

"Hell," said Butch, "he ain't got rabies or nothing. What you going to do, Tommy?"

"We're going to fifteen Belmont Street."

"But you can't—"

"The hell I can't."

But they didn't go there direct. They stopped off at Farrell's room and Farrell came back to the car with a big black pot and an alarm clock.

"What are you going to do with that?" said Butch.

"When I was south a few months ago, I heard a funny story. And I'm not laughing about it. Let's go."

At fifteen Belmont Street, the manager, Mr. Harrison, met them very graciously, rubbing his hands. "What can I do for you gentlemen? Any testimony..."

"I want to see Meyers' apartment," said Farrell.

Butch looked back toward the car where they had left Toto. "Don't you want—" he began.

"Right away," thundered Farrell.

Harrison took them up to the rooms and stood waiting their pleasure.

"Now bring down that Murphy guy," said Farrell.

When Harrison had departed, Farrell went to work. With ruthless hands he began to strip the top from the fireplace, but he found nothing there. He went all along the floorboards and again found nothing. Harrison was just returning when Farrell discovered an extra compartment in the kitchenette cooler.

Murphy looked very nervous. His small red face was redder than ever, and he wiped his hands ceaselessly upon his laboratory apron.

"If you gentlemen think—" began Murphy.

"I'll do the talking," said Farrell. He pointed at the cooking pot he had upended on the table. The ticking of the alarm clock came loudly from within.

"That thing," said Farrell, "is something I invented myself, and I want to see right now if it works. Due to the odd circumstances of this case, I want to question you gentlemen."

Murphy looked startled.

"This thing," continued Farrell, in spite of Butch's surprised gaze, "is a lie detector of an unusual sort. It's wired so that the added heat . . . But then, there's no need of explaining it. An alarm rings under it when a man lies."

"My dear officer," said Murphy, "I—"

Farrell grabbed Murphy by the arms and swung him around so that Murphy's body hid the pot from view.

Farrell stepped back. "Now, Doctor, place your finger on that pot and answer this question: Did you kill Meyers?"

Murphy shrugged and said, "No."

"That's all right," said Farrell. "I know you didn't. Now you, Harrison, as a matter of form—I'm going to take every man in this house—you put your finger on that pot and turn your back to me."

Harrison did so.

Farrell said, "Did you kill Meyers?"

"No," said Harrison.

"That's all right," said Farrell. "Turn around."

"What the hell?" said the mystified Butch.

Farrell was smiling thinly. "Gentlemen," said Farrell, "let's see your hands."

Instantly the two men understood. Murphy smiled and displayed a blackened index finger. But Harrison leaped away with a cry of fear.

Butch tripped the man and grasped his wrists. Butch held up all the white fingers. "He didn't touch it," said Butch.

"You," said Farrell, pointing inexorably at Harrison, "killed Meyers. Butch, go get Toto."

Harrison was shaking when Farrell forced him back into a chair, but Harrison's lips were tightly compressed. Murphy was chuckling about the lie detector.

Toto was brought in a moment and wagged his plumy tail at the sight of Murphy. And then all of Toto's imperial blood began to boil. A snarl was funny coming from such a little dog, but Toto meant it. Harrison cringed back.

"That's the ticket, mutt," said Farrell. He was smiling now, a thousand years lifted off his age.

"Hold Harrison here," said Farrell, and went away.

A full hour later he came back, tagged by the janitor. In

Farrell's hand was a sack, and in the sack was seventy-five thousand dollars in cash.

"You killed Meyers for this dough, Harrison," said Farrell, "and it may go easier with you if you talk. I'll tell you why I've got the goods on you.

"The lieutenant found that Meyers was a miserly guy. You told me yourself the night we came here that you didn't have a key to Meyers' door. Well, you did have a key, but you'd just had it made and you didn't want Meyers to know that you had it.

"You forced your way into Murphy's laboratory and stole a needleful of rabies culture. Then you sneaked into Meyers' room when the old man was asleep and his niece was on the switchboard, and you knocked him over the head. That done, you injected the culture into Meyers' hand, took Toto here and forced his teeth through the flesh. That's how Toto picked up those germs—but they were on his teeth and didn't take effect.

"You fed Toto something to make him very sick and then you stepped outside and phoned headquarters about a mad dog. You didn't want it to go through the switchboard because June Beach would have gone to get her dog before we could have gotten here. She didn't know about it.

"You thought about the switchboard because you own the house. Another man wouldn't have. You knew old Meyers had dough hidden here which even his niece didn't know about. You suspected it and spied upon him, but you had to kill him to steal it—or so you thought.

"And I just now found this bag of money in your apartment and the janitor is the witness."

And though it first appeared to be a very flimsy case, Harrison confessed without any third degree at all; and besides, the lieutenant knew that it's impossible to convict a girl who loves her dog, and the lieutenant easily saw that the case would have to lie as it was, or Farrell would lie as to how it might have been.

And so Harrison burned for the mad dog murder, and now Farrell is on the homicide squad, solving murders right and left. And Butch Hanlon sometimes drives Farrell to the scene of a crime, but now it's Farrell that complains.

Farrell says, "For God's sakes, Butch, slow down. Can'tcha remember that I've got a wife and dog at home?"

The Blow Torch Murder

The Blow Torch Murder

THE crime which the papers played up as the blow torch murder occurred, so it seems, at six o'clock that spring evening, though it was not discovered until six the following dawn, much to the disgust of Ham Logan the homicide veteran.

Springtime was rather trying for Ham. He was sleepy enough for ten months of the year, but in spring . . . !

That afternoon, a couple hours before the announced time of the killing, Ham Logan was stretched out on a bench, his derby hat tilted over and hiding his small eyes and fat jowls, but revealing his open mouth from which came sonorous symphonies of pure enjoyment. His hands were folded across his paunch and gently rose and fell in perfect time.

All in all it was a very peaceful scene. The sergeant at the desk had his feet higher than his head, his collar was open and he dozed blissfully to the accompaniment of the twittering birds outside the station house.

At four o'clock, crime raised its ugly face in the form of Weasel Martin.

Weasel Martin was thin, quite able to squeeze through cell bars. He was dressed in a checkered vest, a black coat and light-colored pants. He swung a cane and tried to look repentant.

Weasel Martin rapped sharply on the desk to wake up the sergeant. Ham Logan shoved back his derby and sat up, blinking at this unheard-of appearance. The sergeant lowered his feet and scowled to hide the fact that he had been asleep.

"I just stole a car," said Weasel Martin impatiently.

The sergeant looked at Ham and Ham looked at the Weasel.

"Since when," said Ham, "did you get so law-abiding as to steal cars?"

"Never mind when. I stole it all right."

The sergeant yelled for a harness bull and when that worthy had lumbered into the room, the sergeant said, "Check up and see if Weasel's lying. Meantime, lock him up."

The Weasel, still trying to look sad, was led off to the cells. Ham Logan scratched his head for a while and then began to slump down for another forty winks.

At four-thirty Chink Edwards came bustling in, very much in a hurry. He looked rumpled and his slant eyes were as shifty as ever. He was pasty white.

"What do you do with guys who break windows?" said the Chink.

The sergeant pulled himself awake, lowered his feet and blinked. Ham Logan raised his derby and peered under the black brim.

"I said I broke a window," repeated the Chink. "Whatcha going to do about it?"

Ham Logan grunted, "*You* broke a window? I thought you were in the numbers racket."

"Beat it," said the sergeant.

"You mean . . ." spluttered the Chink, "that you ain't got

any more respect for the citizens of this town than to let them go around breaking windows every time they feel like it?"

The sergeant scowled horribly and yelled for another harness bull. "Lock him up and see about it," said the sergeant. "The Chink says he broke a window."

The Chink was led off toward the cells.

"Hm," said Ham Logan. "Looks like a convention."

Neither of them had time to settle themselves. Papa Johnson and Joey the Mick wandered in and looked the place over with critical eyes. Papa Johnson looked like a turtle with his long hooked nose and his oversized collar. Joey the Mick was wearing a brilliant yellow suit and a purple silk shirt and a tan derby. They both smiled and bobbed their heads in greeting.

"What the hell is this?" said Ham Logan. "Old Home Week?"

"We heard—" began Papa Johnson.

"We just beat up Flossie, the Chink's girl," said Joey the Mick. "You still arrest guys for assault and battery here?"

"Ow," said Ham Logan. "Has the Salvation Army been around or what? Who cares what happens to the Chink's moll, huh? G'wan, beat it."

"You mean," said Papa Johnson reprovingly, "that you allow our fair city to become stained with woman-beaters? You mean you won't uphold the worthy statutes of the state?"

"That from a snow peddler?" said Ham. "Wait until we catch up with you, Papa. You'll find out all about jails then. I thought you had a smart mouthpiece with you. He wouldn't worry about beating up a dame. What's the racket?"

Neither Joey the Mick nor Papa Johnson had anything to say.

The sergeant called out another officer and instructed him to lock up both of the newcomers.

"Wait a minute," said Ham Logan. "Where's Dude MacFarlane? What's the idea, anyway?"

"Perhaps my lawyer," said Papa Johnson, "will be here a little later. At present, gentlemen, pray do your duty."

They too were led away, leaving Ham Logan sitting up straight and frowning darkly.

"Something funny about this," said Ham. "Just you wait. All hell's going to pop loose."

"Think so? Maybe they suddenly got a conscience or something."

"Conscience! Those guys would cut off a kid's hand to get a stick of candy, any one of them. What's the gag?"

It puzzled him not a little, but soon the spring air stole over them and the twittering birds lulled them and they dozed on, waiting for the six o'clock shift.

At six nothing had happened, but Ham stayed around until midnight, sleeping on the hard benches and in the chairs, waiting.

At twelve o'clock a lawyer named Lambert bustled into the station with a briefcase and an air of preoccupation. The new desk sergeant looked between the white globes at him.

"You've got four or five men in here," said the lawyer. "I want them out."

"Who do you mean?" said the sergeant.

"Martin, Edwards, Johnson and Joey the Mick. They haven't done anything."

Ham Logan woke up in the corner and pried the derby off his face. He approached the lawyer. "I thought Dude MacFarlane was their mouthpiece."

"I have been called. That is all I know. What are the charges?"

The sergeant looked over the daybook and discovered that Weasel Martin was wanted for stealing a car, that Chink Edwards had broken a window, and that Papa Johnson and Joey the Mick had beaten up a woman.

"Have you made any investigation of these charges?" said Lambert.

The sergeant looked through the day's reports, growing more and more puzzled. "Why, no. No stolen cars have been reported, Haines couldn't find a broken window in the whole town. What's this all about, Lambert?"

Lambert looked toward the door. The girl named Flossie came in, walking with greasy hips.

"Tell these gentlemen you haven't been touched," said Lambert.

"Who do ya mean?" said Flossie.

"Tell them," said Lambert, "that you didn't see Papa Johnson and Joey the Mick all day."

"Those dear boys? Why, of course not," said Flossie.

"Huh," snapped Ham, "keep them in on principle. They got it coming."

"I can't do that," said the sergeant. "They . . . Isn't there something I could hold them on? Disrespect to the law or—"

"I don't know of anything, damn it," replied Ham.

"Let 'em out," said the sergeant to an officer.

73

It was exactly one o'clock when Weasel Martin, Chink Edwards, Papa Johnson and Joey the Mick filed out of the station. They told Ham Logan goodbye very politely when they went. Flossie gave Ham a cheap smile and followed them.

"Well," said Ham, "there's nothing I can do." He yawned noisily and adjusted his derby. "I'm going home and get some sleep."

The body was found at six the next morning, and at five minutes after six the phone beside Ham Logan's bed knifed his slumbers with its raucous roar.

"Hello," yawned Ham.

"Desk," said the receiver. "Get over to the Hanover Hotel right away. You know more about this than anyone else."

"Know more about what?" sighed Ham. "Honest, I don't know anything, and besides, six is a hell of a time—"

"Dude MacFarlane's been murdered."

"I knew it, I knew it," wailed Ham. "Something was bound to happen just when— What else?"

"Go on over and find out."

Ham Logan peeled off his nightshirt, put on his derby and dressed. He staggered out into the half-light of spring and took a trolley car to the Hanover Hotel.

Two men were waiting there for him. He shoved them aside and took the elevator. Another man stood outside the room twiddling his nightstick.

"In there," said the officer.

"Anybody here yet?"

"Not yet."

Ham went in. Dude MacFarlane was dead, no question about it whatever. He was sprawled in the center of the room, arms outflung, black mouth gaping, sleek hair still sleek, black eyes wide open.

In life the man had been slender, even lean, but now his stomach was grotesquely swollen under his torn evening shirt, as though about to explode.

"Poison?" said Ham. "Or . . ."

Ham walked around the body. He moved sluggishly as though his shoes were made of lead. He sighed deeply and sat down in an easy chair to wait for the headquarters gang and the coroner. There was nothing he could do before they came.

The door slammed open and activity and noise rushed into the room. The coroner was followed by a fingerprint man, a photographer, and five reporters who eagerly sent their pencils flying.

Blake, the coroner, nodded to Ham. "Done anything?"

"Waiting for you," said Ham. "Let's get this thing over with."

Blake, conscientious as any coroner should be and although not required by law to do any detecting, was anxious to help out. He knelt beside the corpse and as a formality, placed his stethoscope against MacFarlane's chest.

"Dead," said Blake. He examined the dead man's mouth, playing a flashlight into it. "Corrosive action on the flesh. My God, Ham, it looks like this guy swallowed a keg of molten steel. Tissue all burned up as far down as I can see."

Ham looked about the floor and picked up a blow torch which lay in a pile of burned matches. The fingerprint man dusted it and found glove marks only.

"It would appear," said Ham, "that they turned this blow torch down his throat. That right?"

"Yes, that would do it. Hell of a way to die. Blue flame didn't even blacken his teeth, but it charred his tongue. Ate up most of his throat, too. Blow torch seems to be the answer."

Blake looked the body over. "No marks of violence at all. Whoever did it just held him and squirted fire down his throat. Killed him instantly." He tapped the taut and swollen stomach. "But this looks like it might be poison of some kind. Have to have a thorough autopsy, of course. Still, hot flame shot into a man's insides would be apt to puff him up quite a bit. Ventilating system must be good in here. Otherwise the odor would drive us out."

"Thanks," said Ham. "Now listen," and his voice took on the tone of a prayer, "how long has he been dead?"

"We can determine that two or three ways," said Blake. "Post-mortem rigidity would be delayed a little, I think, by this applied heat. Make it four hours minimum time. Now . . ." He took a clinical thermometer from his bag and took MacFarlane's body temperature.

"Body heat eighty-seven. Room about seventy. A little higher because of this blow torch." Blake scowled for a moment and then said judicially, "That looks like he's been dead eleven or twelve hours. But wait a minute, let me try something else."

Ham sighed deeply. So far it looked like Dude MacFarlane had been killed between six and nine the evening before, and if that were so, then what a hell of a case this would be!

Blake made some preliminary coagulation tests. The dead man's blood was thick and heavy, clinging to the applied horse hairs and dragging them.

"I think I am right," said Blake. "He was killed eleven or twelve hours ago. I'll make a thorough autopsy for poison. That swollen stomach looks suspicious." He packed his things into his black bag. "That all you want, Ham?"

"Got the pictures?" Ham asked the photographer. "Okay, take it out. I'm going to stay around here for a little while and think. Wait a minute." He leaned over the corpse and unfastened an expensive watch from the stiff wrist. "Now go ahead."

"Since when did you start stiff-frisking?" said Blake, smiling.

"I wanna see," said Ham, "whether dead men wind watches."

The apartment was cleared and Ham wandered through the rooms, looking things over.

In a closet, on the floor, he found a white vest which contained a few coins and a cigarette lighter. He brought it out to the light and examined it.

"That's funny," said Ham, removing his derby and scratching the few hairs which remained on his otherwise lacquered pate. "That's funny as hell."

He laid it on the desk for future reference and then turned his attention to Dude MacFarlane's files. A small strongbox had been forced open. Not even dust remained. Ham went to all the deep ashtrays in the apartment and discovered a fluttery heap of black paper ash in each.

"Records," he decided. "Incriminating records."

The easy chair beckoned to him. He sank luxuriously into its depths and pulled the phone over to him. He called headquarters.

"Round up Chink Edwards, Papa Johnson, Joey the Mick and Weasel Martin," said Ham. "Hold 'em for questioning."

"Okay, Ham. How's it going?"

"I feel like a squirrel trying to crack a cast-iron nut," sighed Ham.

He rang off and called the morgue. "Hello, have you got MacFarlane's corpse there? Yeah? Well, listen, go into the autopsy room and see what kind of a vest he was wearing. . . . Yeah, is that so? A black vest. Thanks. Gimme that autopsy report as soon as you can."

He eyed the white vest on the desk for a full minute and then muttered, "He'd know better than that. Y'don't wear a black vest with a tail coat. You wear a white vest—or Dude MacFarlane would."

Ham took the blow torch out with him and approached the nearest hardware store. Yes, that was a Vesuvius torch. Only one store in town carried them.

Ham took himself there and found that the store was a narrow affair set between dingy houses, fronted by an entanglement of red rakes, dusty garden hose, watering cans and brooms with green and yellow handles.

The proprietor came out rubbing his hands when the dinner bell tinkled over the door. He was small, hunched over, and he wore a round cloth cap squarely on his gray locks. He adjusted his gold-rimmed glasses and saw that Ham carried a blow torch.

"This was bought here, wasn't it?" said Ham.

"Yes, yes . . . it's a Vesuvius torch. But what's the matter, huh? I can't give no money back. It's been used!" He eyed Ham for a moment. "But maybe I could give half, huh? I hope it gave satisfaction. If it—"

"It gave satisfaction all right," said Ham. He flipped open his shiny dark coat and showed the proprietor the badge. "I want to know who bought it."

"Oh . . . aw . . . why, yes, I maybe got a sales slip. I only sold one like this in six months. You wait right here."

Ham sank down on a keg of rusty nails and waited patiently. Soon the proprietor came back with the sales slip. Ham took it from him. "Can't you remember the guy that bought it?"

"Sure, sure. I remember him fine." Ham waited, fearing to breathe. Here was the clue and the case. The hardware man added, "A messenger boy. He was a little feller with—"

"Rats," said Ham, disgustedly. "There are ten thousand in town. But look here, he also got a thermos bottle. How about that?"

"That's right. A small thermos bottle."

Ham stuffed the slip in his pocket and went out. He took a trolley car back to headquarters.

The sergeant took his feet off his desk. "I got the quartet for you, Ham. They're singing soprano, plenty. Anything turn up?"

79

"I dunno," said Ham. He sat down at his own desk and took up the phone.

"You got that autopsy yet?" he asked the morgue.

"Pretty near," replied Blake. "I'm hanging around. No poison, though. That's out. I been trying—"

"Still say he was dead twelve hours?"

"According to coagulation, I think so. At least the report on this autopsy would stand in court. He had blood clots in his arteries as big as your thumb, and—"

"Forget it," said Ham. "What about that bloated stomach?"

"Nothing to it. Just hot air, that's all. They shoved the blow torch down his throat and the air was forced along with the flame. About the time he's been dead, I might mention that an extreme condition such as terrific heat would hasten the coagulation and make it appear—"

"You don't mean it?" said Ham sitting eagerly forward. "Then there's a chance that he wasn't dead more than—"

"You're wrong," replied Blake. "In a case of this sort it is necessary to fall back on body temperature and I found out he was eighty-seven degrees. That means, what with this coagulation and all, that he was dead twelve hours. There's no getting around that."

"All right," said Ham, wearily, hanging up.

He made his way down to the bullpen. Excited voices could be heard, but when Ham entered, the quartet turned to him with smiles.

"Nice shirt you've got there," said Ham to Joey the Mick.

Joey the Mick vainly touched his purple silk. "Yeah, ain't it? I got one for every day in the week."

"Is that so?" said Ham, astounded. "Ever wear tail coats and things?"

"Whadda I want with tail coats?"

"I thought so," said Ham. "By the way, have any of you boys been on Sunday School picnics lately?"

Four heads told him no very seriously.

"Then what do you want with a thermos bottle?"

They grinned at him and said nothing. Their expressions plainly inferred that he was crazy.

Ham shoved back his derby hat, pried his thumbs under his suspenders and glowered at them. "Listen, you mugs, I don't want to have to go over you with a rubber hose. MacFarlane was your lawyer. He had the goods on you and tried blackmail, didn't he?"

Four mouths, in various stages of distortion, remained soundless.

"Come on, what did you do it for?"

"You infer," said Papa Johnson haughtily, "that we murdered him? Why should we? A fine, upright pillar of the law, MacFarlane."

"Then why did you have Lambert spring you?"

"A cheaper job," said Joey the Mick.

"MacFarlane costs dough," added Weasel Martin, dusting a speck from his extremely cut blue coat.

Lambert came puffing with writs and insistence. "Now look here, Logan, this thing has gone far enough. You can't hold these men for murder."

Ham merely looked at him.

"I have here all the necessary papers," added Lambert. "You

have no evidence against these men. I am fully cognizant of the details of this case. MacFarlane was killed between six and nine last night with a blow torch. All four of these men, according to your own books, were in this station from four-thirty or so until midnight last night. They could not have murdered MacFarlane. The thing is simple."

"Too damned simple," said Ham.

"Then let them out instantly. You can't hold them for murder."

"I ain't holding 'em for murder," said Ham, snapping his suspenders. "They're here as material witnesses."

"But how could they witness—?"

"You never can tell," said Ham and walked thoughtfully away.

He went to his office and sat down in his specially upholstered swivel chair. He put his feet on the desk and hauled the phone to him.

"Hello, Blake there? Well, listen Blake, you still sure MacFarlane—"

"Damn it, what's the matter with you? Won't you take no for an answer? MacFarlane was murdered between six and nine last night. The coagulation and the body temperature showed that. We couldn't find a bit of poison in his body. The corrosive action of the tissue—"

"What'd his guts look like?" said Ham.

"Black," snapped Blake. "Black as coal. The whole stomach and the esophagus were fried—even part of the lungs."

"Is that so?" said Ham.

"Yes, that's so. And in case you forget again, MacFarlane was killed between six and nine last night."

"Okay," said Ham docilely and hung up.

He placed the blow torch before him and pumped it up. Then he opened the valve, let the gasoline run for a moment and finally lit up. The torch roared hoarsely.

The lieutenant shoved his red nose into the office. "Hey, I thought you was working on the MacFarlane case."

"I am," defended Ham.

"Well, what are you doin' playing with that blow torch? You'll burn the whole place down."

The lieutenant notwithstanding, Ham let the torch run for fifteen minutes and then shut it off. Locking his office and leaving the blow torch behind him, he went down to the corner beanery and, perching upon a rickety stool, consumed a hot roast-beef sandwich, three cups of coffee and two pieces of pie.

He went back to the torch and felt it hopefully. It was red hot. He phoned the desk. "Wake me up in about two hours, will you?"

"Okay, Ham."

Ham tipped back in the swivel chair, placed his bulldog-toed shoes on his desk, tilted forward his hard-boiled hat, folded his hands across his comfortable stomach and dozed peacefully. A homeless fly came and explored his mouth. A large June bug methodically smashed out its brains against the windowpane.

The phone rang and Ham thanked the desk. He felt of the torch and found it very cold.

"Well," he said, "that didn't get me anyplace, did it?"

He took MacFarlane's watch out of his pocket and laid it beside the torch. The square face was gold and the hands had a diamond chip in each.

That done, he again adjusted himself in his chair, folded his hands and again went to sleep.

About six o'clock the lieutenant looked in and coughed hard enough to shake the walls. Ham came slowly awake and lowered his feet, almost knocking the watch off the desk.

"Say, Logan, you know what I heard this morning?" The lieutenant paused for effect. "I heard that a guy named Dude MacFarlane was murdered and that another guy named Logan was supposed to be on the case. D'you hear anything about it?"

"Oh, yes," said Ham. "I'm working on it now."

The lieutenant left his scowl hanging heavily in the room. Ham went down to the beanery and had a double order of ham and eggs. He sopped the yellow up with his bread and indulged himself in four slices of apple pie. Then he washed everything down with a third cup of coffee and went back to his office.

For a time he was very busy. He wrote:

Things I ought to believe:

MacFarlane was killed with a blow torch.

He was killed just when he was starting out for a good time.

That he was dead twelve hours.

That the four mugs were in jail when it happened.

When he considered this, he wrote another list, a somewhat idiotic group of words which apparently meant nothing in particular.

Black—white
Night—morning
Time—watch
Up—down
Red—green
Hot—cold
Paper—ashes
Back—forth

He put the purloined watch under the light beside the blow torch and then, shrugging himself into a more comfortable position, once more went to sleep.

At three o'clock that morning, Ham Logan went down to the desk. The sergeant looked up.

"Book Chink Edwards, Weasel Martin, Papa Johnson and Joey the Mick for murder," said Ham.

"What the hell? I thought."

Ham saw Lambert coming then. Ham walked down the halls to the cells and routed out the four.

"I didn't want to keep you in suspense," said Ham to the quartet. "You're booked for MacFarlane's murder."

"What the hell do you mean?" snarled the Weasel.

"You can't do that," snapped Chink Edwards.

"We were all in jail when it happened!" cried Joey the Mick.

"My dear sir," said Papa Johnson, "you are utterly insane!"

*"I didn't want to keep you in suspense," said Ham to the quartet.
"You're booked for MacFarlane's murder."*

"Look here, flatfoot," blustered Lambert, "you're overstepping yourself. You haven't any proof of this thing."

"I haven't, huh?" grunted Ham. "Well, dead men don't wind watches for one thing. This watch stopped ten minutes ago. If MacFarlane had been killed between six and nine night before last, he wouldn't have had time to wind this watch, would he? Everybody winds watches when they go to bed and night-owl MacFarlane never turned in until dawn. But he *did* wind it, so he was killed early *yesterday* morning, maybe about 3:00 AM."

"That's no proof!" howled Lambert. "You can't make it stick."

"Rats," said Ham. "You guys are dumb. You walked in here and gave yourself up for a perfect alibi. Well, MacFarlane wasn't dead until after you got sprung."

"But the coroner—"

"We ain't arguing this in court," said Ham, "but I want to let you guys know you ain't so smart. Blow torch, hell. MacFarlane wasn't killed with a blow torch, he was killed with a thermos bottle.

"You guys got scared. You thought MacFarlane had too much on you. You had to kill him and burn his papers. After we let you out, you went up to his apartment, about 3:00 or 4:00 AM, pulled him out of bed and murdered him. Then you put his evening clothes on him to make it look like it'd been done earlier. But you didn't know that guys wear white vests with tail coats.

"His stomach was all swollen up, wasn't it? Blake said it had air in it only. Well, that was enough. I just called

Blake and checked this with him. Extreme conditions make the blood coagulate faster, fixing a different time of death. MacFarlane was colder than he should have been. He was only dead a couple hours when we found him and yet he'd lost twelve degrees, see?"

"That doesn't prove—" began Lambert.

"Rats, you wanted us to believe he was killed with heat. He was opposites in everything, why not that? You guys poured liquid air down his throat, and that's almost a hundred and ninety degrees below zero centigrade. It froze the guy's throat and stomach instantly, meat freezing black, and then gradually passed off into regular air, leaving no trace at all, just swelling up his stomach—because the stuff expands about five hundred times, or maybe fifteen hundred or something.

"All of which, like burning, comes under the head of corrosive action, coagulating the blood quicker and cooling the body like he'd been soaked in ice water.

"I dunno how you mugs figured all that out. I guess it was you, huh, Papa Johnson? Well, you weren't smart enough to change his clothes right or to steal his watch. And you forgot the air would swell up his stomach when it evaporated, and you forgot to cover your tracks on that thermos bottle.

"You took the thermos bottle away and left the blow torch, see? And thermos bottles is what they use to carry liquid air, it boiling off so easy."

Ham adjusted his hard-boiled hat, rocked a little on his heels and grinned. But the grin faded into a yawn and he walked away, leaving the quartet wilted and goggle-eyed, clinging to the bars.

"Expect a dead man to wind a watch, huh?" said Ham to the desk, elaborately rubbing his eyes. "Well, it's been a long day. I guess," he sighed, "that I better get home and get me some sleep."

Story Preview

NOW that you've just ventured through some of the captivating tales in the Stories from the Golden Age collection by L. Ron Hubbard, turn the page and enjoy a preview of *Brass Keys to Murder*. Join Navy Lieutenant Stephen Craig, who's being pursued for a murder he didn't commit and must find the culprits to prove his innocence. When his search crosses paths with a set of brass keys that may match a trove of Chinese treasure chests, he follows a trail to a dockside warehouse—where the real killers lie in wait.

Brass Keys to Murder

L IEUTENANT Stephen Craig, attired in white duty belt
and blue serge uniform, leaned against the rail of the
USS *Burnham* and watched the shore boat come out toward
him through the fog. The muffled stutter of its exhaust grew
clearer.

Steve Craig, at present officer of the deck, was interested
in the shore boat only because it alone was moving in this
quiet harbor. The bluish landing light fell upon his features,
showing them to be big and rugged. His jaw was as square as
a clipper's mainsail and his eyes were the shade of an arctic
sea. His white-topped cap was set over one ear, and its golden
spread eagle was tarnished by the impacts of many seas and
the dampness of countless fogs—fogs of the Thames, the
Huangpu, Colón.

He was obviously a destroyer man, bearing the stamp of
lurching, giddy decks, smashing waves and full speed ahead.

The shore boat, a chunky affair, rapped against the landing
stage, bobbing in the gentle, greasy swell. A man dressed in
dirty dungarees held the lines and tried to aid the person who
stepped out.

Steve Craig's brows lifted in surprise. A girl had bridged
the gap and her high-heeled slippers were pounding up the
spotless ladder toward the deck. She glanced up, displaying a

small, well-set face presided over by a pair of great dark eyes which were deep and liquid and troubled.

"Sally!" Steve cried. "What's the idea of coming out here this time of night?"

She clattered on up and the shore boat swung away, heading back to the docks. Sally's small hand fastened on a stanchion.

"I know you've got the duty, Steve, and that I shouldn't be here, but . . . but this is serious. You've got to get away from here. I've brought some money and you can run before they come."

"Run! Before who comes? Quiet down, child, and tell me—"

"Steve, your father died tonight. He . . . he was murdered!"

"Murdered! My father? But . . . why, I've got to get ashore right away! I can get somebody to relieve me. I'll call for a boat and we'll—"

"No, Steve. They're coming up here—the police, I mean. And they . . . they're going to arrest you for the murder!"

"*Me!*" Steve's eyes widened with amazement. "But why should I want to kill Dad?"

"They know that you and your father didn't get along, Steve, and that—"

"But, Sally! We patched that all up weeks ago, just before he sailed for Panama on his last trip. He was coming out here tonight to see me. Just got in this afternoon, and I've had the watch all day—all afternoon, I mean."

"Have you any letters from him or anything like that to show that you patched everything up?"

"No . . . he never wrote to anybody. Sally, they can't pin this thing on me. Why, I've been right here on this deck since noon!"

"But who's been with you since five o'clock?"

"Nobody much. Billy Reynolds came up and talked for a while and then went ashore. Most of the crew is on liberty, and it's been too foggy to stay up on deck tonight for movies. The quartermaster isn't feeling so good, and I let him go down to the sick bay an hour or so ago."

"Can't you get someone to say... look, Steve! Here comes the police launch! You haven't time to do anything. They'll make you—"

The harbor patrol boat, its stern crowded with men, shoved out of the black mist and banged hard against the landing stage, making the platform creak. Men began to get out. Each time one reached the stage, he looked up at the deck, cautiously, before he clambered up the ladder. There were four in all. Haggarty, Detective-Sergeant Green and two officers. The boat swung away to circle and wait.

Green stepped down to the curving steel deck and looked around, mouthing a cigar. His overcoat collar was turned up and his small eyes were set far back in the folds of his face.

"Hello, Craig," he said. "I'm afraid you'll have to come along with us. There's a little matter—oh, beg pardon, Miss Randolph," he said, tipping his hard hat. "I see you got here with the news before we did. Know all about it, do you, Craig? How we found the body, I mean."

"I only know that my father is dead."

"Of course I expected you to claim ignorance of the works—they always do. You'd better come along with us right now. We'll put you in out of this fog where you won't catch cold."

"You can belay the wisecracks, Green. Let's hear some more about this affair."

Green looked at Steve's arctic eyes and shrugged. "All right. But you're just wasting time, that's all. We found Jeremiah Craig's body about an hour and a half ago, floating near the docks. He got it with a knife in his side. German clasp knife. We pulled him out, and I got busy. I used to have this beat about ten years ago, before they made a sergeant out of me and put me in the homicide squad. And I know all about the fuss you kicked up by running away to the Naval Academy instead of going to a merchant marine school. And you knew all the time how much old Craig hated the Navy."

"You can skip that," said Steve. "How do you figure I killed him? I've been officer of the deck since noon, because we're short of officers. And you know that I haven't left this ship. Look at the log over there if you don't believe me."

Green stepped to the tilted desk and glanced at the huge book which lay open upon it. Coming back to Craig, he worked his cigar over into the corner of his mouth.

"That hasn't anything to do with it," he said. "When old Craig docked this afternoon he heard you were in port. And he decided it was about time he came over and gave you a lacing. And so when you were alone on deck he came up the gangplank swearing at you. And you grabbed out your knife and shoved it into his ribs. It was foggy and it was dark and nobody saw it at all."

"Go on," said Steve grimly.

"I figure it that way because the body was found south from this boat. And the tide was ebbing in that direction three or four hours ago."

"Green," said Steve, "you ought to have been a sailor. As a cop, you're a dud."

"Look here, young fellow—"

"While I'm standing on this deck you'll address me as lieutenant. As to your dumbness—"

Sally Randolph stepped between them. "Don't fight, please."

Steve pushed her gently to one side, without looking at her. "As to your dumbness, Jeremiah Craig and I made up that old quarrel weeks ago. And he wanted to see me this trip to have dinner with me. I saw him on his last cruise."

"Were there any witnesses to that?" barked Green.

"No. We met on the dock late one night."

"Why didn't you knife him that time? Wasn't your alibi good enough?"

"Keep a civil tongue in your head, Green," Steve snapped. "You may think you can come aboard this ship with two armed policemen and a fathead detective and tell me where to head in, but you're half-seas over, get me?" He patted his duty belt and the holstered .45 which dangled from the webbing. The two policemen stepped back, glancing hurriedly down the gangway to make certain that it was clear.

To find out more about *Brass Keys to Murder* and how you can obtain your copy, go to www.goldenagestories.com.

Glossary

STORIES FROM THE GOLDEN AGE *reflect the words and expressions used in the 1930s and 1940s, adding unique flavor and authenticity to the tales. While a character's speech may often reflect regional origins, it also can convey attitudes common in the day. So that readers can better grasp such cultural and historical terms, uncommon words or expressions of the era, the following glossary has been provided.*

---

beetling: frowning; scowling.

belay: stop.

Black Maria: patrol wagon; an enclosed truck or van used by the police to transport prisoners.

bloodhounding: relentlessly pursuing someone or something.

bluecoats: policemen.

bowler: derby; a hard felt hat with a rounded crown and narrow brim, created by James Lock & Co, a firm founded in 1676 in London. The prototype was made in 1850 for a customer of Lock's by Thomas and William Bowler, hat makers in Southwark, England. At first it was dubbed the iron hat because it was hard enough to protect the head, and later picked up the name bowler because of its makers' family name. In the US it became known as a derby from its association with the Kentucky Derby.

bracelets: a pair of handcuffs.

bulldog-toed shoes: shoes with thick soles and high rounded toes.

bullpen: a holding cell where prisoners are confined together temporarily; in the 1800s, jails and holding cells were nicknamed *bullpens,* in respect of many police officers' bullish features—strength and short temper.

bumping off: killing, especially murdering.

burned: to be electrocuted.

cat-and-cream: variation of "the cat that got the cream"; someone who looks very pleased with himself or self-satisfied.

clipper: a very fast sailing ship of the nineteenth century that had multiple masts and square sails.

Colón: a seaport in Panama at the Atlantic end of the Panama Canal.

Colt: an automatic pistol manufactured by the Colt Firearms Company, founded in 1847 by Samuel Colt (1814–1862) who revolutionized the firearms industry with his inventions.

dead to rights: to have enough proof to show that someone has done something wrong.

Fates: the Fates, in classical mythology, are the three goddesses Clotho, Lachesis and Atropos, who control human destiny.

flatfoot: a police officer; cop; a patrolman walking a regular beat.

gangway: a narrow, movable platform or ramp forming a bridge by which to board or leave a ship.

gink: a fellow.

G-men: government men; agents of the Federal Bureau of Investigation.

greasy: fat of body; bulky.

half-seas over: almost drunk.

hard-boiled hat: derby; a man's stiff felt hat with dome-shaped crown and narrow brim.

harness bull: a uniformed police officer.

hell's bells: an interjection indicating irritation, annoyance or surprise.

Huangpu: long river in China flowing through Shanghai. It divides the city into two regions.

juice: electricity, in reference to electrocution for the death penalty.

kerchief: handkerchief.

Limited: a train line making only a limited number of stops en route.

liquid air: air in its liquid state, intensely cold and bluish.

material witness: a witness whose testimony is both relevant to the matter at issue and required in order to resolve the matter.

Mick: term for a person of Irish birth or descent.

moll: a female companion of a gangster.

monk: monkey.

mouthpiece: a lawyer, especially a criminal lawyer.

muff: a short tube of fur or warm cloth, into which hands are placed in order to keep them warm.

mugs: hoodlums; thugs; criminals.

numbers racket: an illegal daily lottery.

Old Home Week: a yearly reunion and celebration lasting a week and consisting of existing and previous residents of a community. This tradition dates back to 1901. The first reunion was held for fifty to sixty men who had previously attended a school together and was called the "Old Boys' Reunion." From there it grew to include the community and its name changed to "Old Home Week."

Palo Alto hat: a wide-brimmed slouch hat with a chinstrap most commonly worn as part of a military uniform, resembling the original Stetson that was called "Boss of the Plains."

pay station: a coin-operated telephone.

peddler: someone who sells illegal drugs to people.

pince-nez: a pair of glasses held on the face by a spring that grips the nose.

puncher: a hired hand who tends cattle and performs other duties on horseback.

roadster: an open-top automobile with a single seat in front for two or three persons, a fabric top and either a luggage compartment or a rumble seat in back. A rumble seat is an upholstered exterior seat with a hinged lid that opens to form the back of the seat when in use.

Rock Creek Park: Rock Creek Park Historic District; a national park reserve in Washington, DC.

rogues' gallery: a set of photographs of known criminals that the police show to crime witnesses for possible identification.

Roman candle: a type of fireworks giving off flaming colored balls and sparks.

rubber hose: a piece of hose made of rubber, used to beat people as a form of torture or in order to obtain a full or partial confession and to elicit information. A rubber hose was used because its blows, while painful, leave only slight marks on the body of the person beaten.

Scheherazade: the female narrator of *The Arabian Nights,* who during one thousand and one adventurous nights saved her life by entertaining her husband, the king, with stories.

singing soprano: being vocal about informing on someone else or confessing to the police.

skullcap: nightcap; a light, close-fitting, brimless cap, usually worn indoors or at night to provide warmth while sleeping.

slug: a bullet.

snow: cocaine or heroin in the form of a white powder.

Stetson: as the most popular broad-brimmed hat in the West, it became the generic name for hat. John B. Stetson was a master hat maker and founder of the company that has been making Stetsons since 1865.

Thames: a river of southern England flowing eastward to a wide estuary on the North Sea. Navigable for large ships as far as London, it is the principal commercial waterway of the country.

trick: shift; the portion of the day scheduled for working.

worthy: an important, honorable person (often used humorously).

Vesuvius: a blow torch model manufactured by the American Stove Company, of St. Louis, Missouri. It is named after an active volcano in southwestern Italy, near Naples.

L. Ron Hubbard
in the Golden Age
of Pulp Fiction

*In writing an adventure story
a writer has to know that he is adventuring
for a lot of people who cannot.
The writer has to take them here and there
about the globe and show them
excitement and love and realism.
As long as that writer is living the part of an
adventurer when he is hammering
the keys, he is succeeding with his story.*

*Adventuring is a state of mind.
If you adventure through life, you have a
good chance to be a success on paper.*

*Adventure doesn't mean globe-trotting,
exactly, and it doesn't mean great deeds.
Adventuring is like art.
You have to live it to make it real.*

—*L. RON HUBBARD*

L. Ron Hubbard
and American
Pulp Fiction

B ORN March 13, 1911, L. Ron Hubbard lived a life at
least as expansive as the stories with which he enthralled
a hundred million readers through a fifty-year career.

Originally hailing from Tilden, Nebraska, he spent his
formative years in a classically rugged Montana, replete with
the cowpunchers, lawmen and desperadoes who would later
people his Wild West adventures. And lest anyone imagine
those adventures were drawn from vicarious experience, he
was not only breaking broncs at a tender age, he was also
among the few whites ever admitted into Blackfoot society
as a bona fide blood brother. While if only to round out an
otherwise rough and tumble youth, his mother was that rarity
of her time—a thoroughly educated woman—who introduced
her son to the classics of Occidental literature even before his
seventh birthday.

But as any dedicated L. Ron Hubbard reader will attest, his
world extended far beyond Montana. In point of fact, and as the
son of a United States naval officer, by the age of eighteen he
had traveled over a quarter of a million miles. Included therein
were three Pacific crossings to a then still mysterious Asia, where
he ran with the likes of Her British Majesty's agent-in-place

L. Ron Hubbard, left, at Congressional Airport, Washington, DC, 1931, with members of George Washington University flying club.

for North China, and the last in the line of Royal Magicians from the court of Kublai Khan. For the record, L. Ron Hubbard was also among the first Westerners to gain admittance to forbidden Tibetan monasteries below Manchuria, and his photographs of China's Great Wall long graced American geography texts.

Upon his return to the United States and a hasty completion of his interrupted high school education, the young Ron Hubbard entered George Washington University. There, as fans of his aerial adventures may have heard, he earned his wings as a pioneering barnstormer at the dawn of American aviation. He also earned a place in free-flight record books for the longest sustained flight above Chicago. Moreover, as a roving reporter for *Sportsman Pilot* (featuring his first professionally penned articles), he further helped inspire a generation of pilots who would take America to world airpower.

Immediately beyond his sophomore year, Ron embarked on the first of his famed ethnological expeditions, initially to then untrammeled Caribbean shores (descriptions of which would later fill a whole series of West Indies mystery-thrillers). That the Puerto Rican interior would also figure into the future of Ron Hubbard stories was likewise no accident. For in addition to cultural studies of the island, a 1932–33

LRH expedition is rightly remembered as conducting the first complete mineralogical survey of a Puerto Rico under United States jurisdiction.

There was many another adventure along this vein: As a lifetime member of the famed Explorers Club, L. Ron Hubbard charted North Pacific waters with the first shipboard radio direction finder, and so pioneered a long-range navigation system universally employed until the late twentieth century. While not to put too fine an edge on it, he also held a rare Master Mariner's license to pilot any vessel, of any tonnage in any ocean.

Yet lest we stray too far afield, there is an LRH note at this juncture in his saga, and it reads in part:

"I started out writing for the pulps, writing the best I knew, writing for every mag on the stands, slanting as well as I could."

To which one might add: His earliest submissions date from the summer of 1934, and included tales drawn from true-to-life Asian adventures, with characters roughly modeled on British/American intelligence operatives he had known in Shanghai. His early Westerns were similarly peppered with details drawn from personal experience. Although therein lay a first hard lesson from the often cruel world of the pulps. His first Westerns were soundly rejected as lacking the authenticity of a Max Brand yarn

Capt. L. Ron Hubbard in Ketchikan, Alaska, 1940, on his Alaskan Radio Experimental Expedition, the first of three voyages conducted under the Explorers Club flag.

(a particularly frustrating comment given L. Ron Hubbard's Westerns came straight from his Montana homeland, while Max Brand was a mediocre New York poet named Frederick Schiller Faust, who turned out implausible six-shooter tales from the terrace of an Italian villa).

Nevertheless, and needless to say, L. Ron Hubbard persevered and soon earned a reputation as among the most publishable names in pulp fiction, with a ninety percent placement rate of first-draft manuscripts. He was also among the most prolific, averaging between seventy and a hundred thousand words a month. Hence the rumors that L. Ron Hubbard had redesigned a typewriter for faster keyboard action and pounded out manuscripts on a continuous roll of butcher paper to save the precious seconds it took to insert a single sheet of paper into manual typewriters of the day.

That all L. Ron Hubbard stories did not run beneath said byline is yet another aspect of pulp fiction lore. That is, as publishers periodically rejected manuscripts from top-drawer authors if only to avoid paying top dollar, L. Ron Hubbard and company just as frequently replied with submissions under various pseudonyms. In Ron's case, the list

A MAN OF MANY NAMES

Between 1934 and 1950, L. Ron Hubbard authored more than fifteen million words of fiction in more than two hundred classic publications. To supply his fans and editors with stories across an array of genres and pulp titles, he adopted fifteen pseudonyms in addition to his already renowned L. Ron Hubbard byline.

*Winchester Remington Colt
Lt. Jonathan Daly
Capt. Charles Gordon
Capt. L. Ron Hubbard
Bernard Hubbel
Michael Keith
Rene Lafayette
Legionnaire 148
Legionnaire 14830
Ken Martin
Scott Morgan
Lt. Scott Morgan
Kurt von Rachen
Barry Randolph
Capt. Humbert Reynolds*

included: Rene Lafayette, Captain Charles Gordon, Lt. Scott Morgan and the notorious Kurt von Rachen—supposedly on the lam for a murder rap, while hammering out two-fisted prose in Argentina. The point: While L. Ron Hubbard as Ken Martin spun stories of Southeast Asian intrigue, LRH as Barry Randolph authored tales of romance on the Western range—which, stretching between a dozen genres is how he came to stand among the two hundred elite authors providing close to a million tales through the glory days of American Pulp Fiction.

L. Ron Hubbard, circa 1930 , at the outset of a literary career that would finally span half a century.

In evidence of exactly that, by 1936 L. Ron Hubbard was literally leading pulp fiction's elite as president of New York's American Fiction Guild. Members included a veritable pulp hall of fame: Lester "Doc Savage" Dent, Walter "The Shadow" Gibson, and the legendary Dashiell Hammett—to cite but a few.

Also in evidence of just where L. Ron Hubbard stood within his first two years on the American pulp circuit: By the spring of 1937, he was ensconced in Hollywood, adopting a Caribbean thriller for Columbia Pictures, remembered today as *The Secret of Treasure Island.* Comprising fifteen thirty-minute episodes, the L. Ron Hubbard screenplay led to the most profitable matinée serial in Hollywood history. In accord with Hollywood culture, he was thereafter continually called

The 1937 Secret of Treasure Island, *a fifteen-episode serial adapted for the screen by L. Ron Hubbard from his novel,* Murder at Pirate Castle.

upon to rewrite/doctor scripts—most famously for long-time friend and fellow adventurer Clark Gable.

In the interim—and herein lies another distinctive chapter of the L. Ron Hubbard story—he continually worked to open Pulp Kingdom gates to up-and-coming authors. Or, for that matter, anyone who wished to write. It was a fairly unconventional stance, as markets were already thin and competition razor sharp. But the fact remains, it was an L. Ron Hubbard hallmark that he vehemently lobbied on behalf of young authors—regularly supplying instructional articles to trade journals, guest-lecturing to short story classes at George Washington University and Harvard, and even founding his own creative writing competition. It was established in 1940, dubbed the Golden Pen, and guaranteed winners both New York representation and publication in *Argosy*.

But it was John W. Campbell Jr.'s *Astounding Science Fiction* that finally proved the most memorable LRH vehicle. While every fan of L. Ron Hubbard's galactic epics undoubtedly knows the story, it nonetheless bears repeating: By late 1938, the pulp publishing magnate of Street & Smith was determined to revamp *Astounding Science Fiction* for broader readership. In particular, senior editorial director F. Orlin Tremaine called for stories with a stronger *human element*. When acting editor John W. Campbell balked, preferring his spaceship-driven tales,

112

Tremaine enlisted Hubbard. Hubbard, in turn, replied with the genre's first truly *character-driven* works, wherein heroes are pitted not against bug-eyed monsters but the mystery and majesty of deep space itself—and thus was launched the Golden Age of Science Fiction.

The names alone are enough to quicken the pulse of any science fiction aficionado, including LRH friend and protégé, Robert Heinlein, Isaac Asimov, A. E. van Vogt and Ray Bradbury. Moreover, when coupled with LRH stories of fantasy, we further come to what's rightly been described as the foundation of every modern tale of horror: L. Ron Hubbard's immortal *Fear.* It was rightly proclaimed by Stephen King as one of the very few works to genuinely warrant that overworked term "classic"—as in: *"This is a classic tale of creeping, surreal menace and horror. . . . This is one of the really, really good ones."*

L. Ron Hubbard, 1948, among fellow science fiction luminaries at the World Science Fiction Convention in Toronto.

To accommodate the greater body of L. Ron Hubbard fantasies, Street & Smith inaugurated *Unknown*—a classic pulp if there ever was one, and wherein readers were soon thrilling to the likes of *Typewriter in the Sky* and *Slaves of Sleep* of which Frederik Pohl would declare: *"There are bits and pieces from Ron's work that became part of the language in ways that very few other writers managed."*

And, indeed, at J. W. Campbell Jr.'s insistence, Ron was regularly drawing on themes from the Arabian Nights and so introducing readers to a world of genies, jinn, Aladdin and Sinbad—all of which, of course, continue to float through cultural mythology to this day.

At least as influential in terms of post-apocalypse stories was L. Ron Hubbard's 1940 *Final Blackout*. Generally acclaimed as the finest anti-war novel of the decade and among the ten best works of the genre ever authored—here, too, was a tale that would live on in ways few other writers imagined. Hence, the later Robert Heinlein verdict: "Final Blackout *is as perfect a piece of science fiction as has ever been written.*"

Portland, Oregon, 1943; L. Ron Hubbard captain of the US Navy subchaser PC 815.

Like many another who both lived and wrote American pulp adventure, the war proved a tragic end to Ron's sojourn in the pulps. He served with distinction in four theaters and was highly decorated for commanding corvettes in the North Pacific. He was also grievously wounded in combat, lost many a close friend and colleague and thus resolved to say farewell to pulp fiction and devote himself to what it had supported these many years—namely, his serious research.

But in no way was the LRH literary saga at an end, for as he wrote some thirty years later, in 1980:

"Recently there came a period when I had little to do. This was novel in a life so crammed with busy years, and I decided to amuse myself by writing a novel that was pure science fiction."

That work was *Battlefield Earth: A Saga of the Year 3000*. It was an immediate *New York Times* bestseller and, in fact, the first international science fiction blockbuster in decades. It was not, however, L. Ron Hubbard's magnum opus, as that distinction is generally reserved for his next and final work: The 1.2 million word *Mission Earth*.

> **Final Blackout**
> *is as perfect a piece of science fiction as has ever been written.*
>
> —Robert Heinlein

How he managed those 1.2 million words in just over twelve months is yet another piece of the L. Ron Hubbard legend. But the fact remains, he did indeed author a ten-volume *dekalogy* that lives in publishing history for the fact that each and every volume of the series was also a *New York Times* bestseller.

Moreover, as subsequent generations discovered L. Ron Hubbard through republished works and novelizations of his screenplays, the mere fact of his name on a cover signaled an international bestseller. . . . Until, to date, sales of his works exceed hundreds of millions, and he otherwise remains among the most enduring and widely read authors in literary history. Although as a final word on the tales of L. Ron Hubbard, perhaps it's enough to simply reiterate what editors told readers in the glory days of American Pulp Fiction:

He writes the way he does, brothers, because he's been there, seen it and done it!

THE STORIES FROM THE GOLDEN AGE

Your ticket to adventure starts here with the Stories from
the Golden Age collection by master storyteller L. Ron Hubbard.
These gripping tales are set in a kaleidoscope of exotic locales and brim
with fascinating characters, including some of the
most vile villains, dangerous dames and brazen heroes
you'll ever get to meet.

The entire collection of over one hundred and fifty stories is being
released in a series of eighty books and audiobooks.
For an up-to-date listing of available titles,
go to www.goldenagestories.com.

AIR ADVENTURE

FAR-FLUNG ADVENTURE

SEA ADVENTURE

TALES FROM THE ORIENT

MYSTERY

FANTASY

SCIENCE FICTION

WESTERN

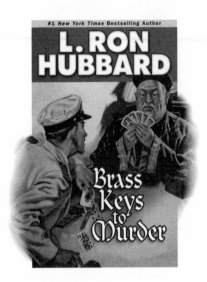

JOIN THE PULP REVIVAL
America in the 1930s and 40s

Pulp fiction was in its heyday and 30 million readers were regularly riveted by the larger-than-life tales of master storyteller L. Ron Hubbard. For this was pulp fiction's golden age, when the writing was raw and every page packed a walloping punch.

That magic can now be yours. An evocative world of nefarious villains, exotic intrigues, courageous heroes and heroines—a world that today's cinema has barely tapped for tales of adventure and swashbucklers.

Enroll today in the Stories from the Golden Age Club and begin receiving your monthly feature edition selected from more than 150 stories in the collection.

You may choose to enjoy them as either a paperback or audiobook for the special membership price of $9.95 each month along with FREE shipping and handling.

CALL TOLL-FREE: **1-877-8GALAXY**
(**1-877-842-5299**) OR GO ONLINE TO
www.goldenagestories.com
AND BECOME PART OF THE PULP REVIVAL!